FAMILY SAYINGS

Books by Natalia Ginzburg

All Our Yesterdays

Family Sayings

The Little Virtues

The City and the House

The Manzoni Family

Valentino and Sagittarius

*Family: Family and Borghesia,
    Two Novellas*

Voices in the Evening

FAMILY
SAYINGS

Revised from the original translation
by D. M. Low

NATALIA GINZBURG

ARCADE PUBLISHING • NEW YORK
Little, Brown and Company

First Arcade paperback edition 1989

Published in the United States by Arcade Publishing, Inc., New York, a Little, Brown company, by arrangement with Seaver books.

Originally published in Italy under the title *Lessico Famigliare*

Library of Congress Cataloging-in-Publication Data
Ginzburg, Natalia.
    [Lessico famigliare. English]
    Family sayings / Natalia Ginzburg : translated
    from the Italian by D.M. Low.
        p.   cm.
    Translation of: Lessico famigliare.
    ISBN 1-55970-027-0
    1. Ginzburg. Natalia—Biography. 2. Authors,
Italian—20th century—Biography. I. Title.
    PQ4817.I5Z4713   1989
    853'.912 — dc20   89-15044
    [B]   CIP

10 9 8 7 6 5 4 3 2 1

BP

PRINTED IN THE UNITED STATES OF AMERICA

Author's Preface

THE places, events and people in this book are all real. I have invented nothing. Every time that I have found myself inventing something in accordance with my old habits as a novelist, I have felt impelled at once to destroy everything thus invented.

The names are real also. In writing this book I could not endure the thought of inventing anything, and therefore I could not alter the actual names, which I felt were an inseparable part of actual persons. Some may possibly not be pleased to find themselves described under their own names. To them I have nothing to say.

I have set down only what I myself could recall. Consequently if this book is read as a chronicle of events it may be objected that there are omissions. Although the book is founded on reality, I think it should be read as though it were a novel, that is, read without demanding of it either more or less than what a novel can offer.

There are also many happenings which I have remembered but have passed over in writing this book. Among them is much which concerned myself directly.

I have had no great wish to speak of myself, since this story is not in fact my own but rather, in spite of all its gaps and omissions, the record of my family. I may add that ever since my childhood and adolescence I have always intended to write a book which would tell the story of the people who lived through those times with me. This is to some extent that book, but only to some extent, because memory is treacherous and books founded on reality are so often only faint reflections and sketches of all that we have seen and heard.

WHEN I was a little girl at home, if one of us children upset a glass at table or dropped a knife, my father's voice bellowed: 'Behave yourself!' If we soaked our bread in the gravy, he cried out, 'Don't lick the plates, don't make messes and slops.'

Messes and slops were things which my father could not stand, any more than he could stand modern pictures.

'You people don't know how to sit at table. You are not people one could take out anywhere. You make such a mess. If you were at a hotel table in England, they would send you out immediately.' He had a very exalted opinion of England, holding it to be the finest example in the world of good breeding.

He used to comment at dinner on the people he had met during the day. He was very severe in his judgments and called them all stupid. 'I thought he was a really silly man,' he would say by way of comment on some new acquaintance. A stage worse than silly men were 'negroes'. A 'negro' for my father was one whose manners were gauche and lacking in assurance; one who dressed inappropriately, who was no good at mountaineering, and was ignorant of foreign languages. Any act or gesture of ours which he thought out of place was classified by him as a '*negrigura*'. 'Don't be "negroes", don't do those *negrigure*,' he shouted at us endlessly. The range of such behaviour was wide: wearing town shoes on expeditions in the mountains; getting into conversation with strangers in a train, or in the street; talking out of the window to one's neighbours; taking off one's shoes in the sitting-room, or warming one's feet at the stove; complaining on our mountaineering expeditions of thirst, fatigue or sore feet; taking rich food on these walks, and napkins for one's fingers.

On our expeditions we were only allowed to take specified kinds of food; cream cheese, jam, pears, and hard-boiled eggs — and we were only allowed to drink tea which he prepared himself on a spirit stove. Frowning the while he would bend his long head, with its bristling red hair, over the stove, and shelter the flame from the wind with the skirts of a woollen rust-coloured jacket,

9

threadbare and torn at the pockets — it was always this same jacket on our holidays in the mountains.

We were never allowed to take with us brandy or lump sugar — 'negro stuff' he would say, and we were not allowed to stop for refreshment at the rest huts, this being decidedly a *negrigura*. So was protecting one's head with a headscarf or a straw hat, or keeping the rain off with a waterproof cap, precautions that were dear to my mother who, in the morning when we were setting out, tried to slip them into the rucksack for us and herself. If my father caught her with them he would throw them angrily away. So there we went, with hobnailed boots, stiff and as heavy as lead, thick socks and woollen caps, dark glasses on our noses and the vertical sun beating on our sweating heads, while we looked with envy on 'the negroes' who went walking in light tennis shoes, or sat at little tables at the chalets devouring cream.

For my mother these expeditions in the mountains were 'the devil's idea of fun for his children'. She always tried to stay at home, above all when it meant eating out of doors. After meals she liked to read the paper and sleep on a sofa behind closed doors.

We always spent the summer in the mountains. We used to take a furnished house for three months, from July to September. Usually they were houses far from other habitation. My father and the other children used to go, with rucksacks on their backs, shopping in the village every day. There was no kind of amusement or distraction. My mother and we children spent the evenings sitting round a table. My father would go off to read on the opposite side of the house; from time to time he put his head in at the door of the room where we were gathered round the table, chattering and playing games. He frowned and looked suspicious, and he would complain to my mother about our servant Natalina who had disarranged some of his books. 'Your dear Natalina,' he would say. 'A lunatic,' he would add, regardless of the fact that Natalina in the kitchen could hear him. In any case Natalina was quite used to the words, 'that lunatic Natalina', and took no offence at all.

Sometimes in the evening my father would prepare for our walks or climbs. Kneeling on the ground he greased his boots and my brothers' with whale fat. He imagined that only he knew how to grease boots properly. Then we heard a loud clatter of iron through the house. He was looking for the crampons, pitons and ice-axes.

10

'Where have you hidden my axe?' he would bellow. 'Lydia, Lydia! where have you hidden my axe?'

He set off for his climbs at four in the morning; sometimes alone, sometimes with a guide with whom he was friendly, and at other times with my brothers and my sister. The day after a climb he was impossible, he was so tired. His face was red and swollen, his lips cracked and bleeding, his nose smeared with a yellow ointment which looked like butter; with knitted brows and furrowed stormy forehead he read the paper without uttering a word, yet a mere trifle was enough to make him explode with terrifying wrath. On returning from a climb with my brothers and sister he would say that they were 'sausages' and 'negroes' and that except for Gino, the eldest, a fine mountaineer, who with a friend did some very difficult climbs, none of his children had inherited his passion for the mountains. My father spoke of Gino and this friend with a mixture of pride and envy, and said that his own wind was no longer so good, since he was growing old.

In any case Gino was his favourite and pleased him in everything. Gino was interested in natural history, collected insects, crystals and other minerals, and was very studious. He went on to read engineering, and when he came home after an examination and said he had passed, my father would ask, 'What do you mean by a pass? How come you have not got a distinction?' And if he did get a pass with distinction, my father would say, 'Pooh, it was an easy examination.'

When it did not suit us to go climbing or on long walks which lasted until the evening, my father still went each day for a 'stroll'. He started early in the morning dressed exactly as for climbing, but without rope, crampons or his ice-axe. He often went alone because our mother and we were, in his own words, 'poltroons', 'sausages' and 'negroes'. He went off with his hands behind his back and his pipe between his teeth, and the heavy tread of his hobnailed boots. Sometimes he compelled my mother to go with him. 'Lydia! Lydia!' he would thunder in the morning, 'Let us go for a walk! You are getting lazy always hanging about in this meadow!' So my mother, being docile, went with him, walking a few paces behind with a light walking-stick and her pullover tied round her waist, and shaking her curly grey hair which she wore very short although my father

11

objected to this fashion. On the day when she had first had her hair cut, his rage was enough to bring the house down. And every time my mother came back from the hairdresser he would exclaim, 'You have had your hair cut again — what an ass you are!' By an 'ass', my father did not mean an ignoramus, but one who did unseemly and tasteless things. We children were 'asses' when we spoke little or answered badly.

'You must have got the idea from Frances,' my father would say to my mother when he noticed that she had cut her hair again. As a matter of fact my father was very fond of my mother's friend Frances and thought highly of her, if for nothing else because she was married to someone who had been his friend from childhood and shared his pursuits. Her one fault in his eyes was that she had introduced my mother to the fashion for short hair. Frances frequently went to Paris where she had relations, and had returned one winter saying, 'Short hair is in in Paris.' 'The fashion in Paris is sporty,' 'The fashion in Paris is sporty,' my sister and my mother repeated all the winter, rather taking the mickey out of Frances, who rolled her 'r's. All our dresses had been shortened and my mother had cut off her hair. My sister did not because she had very lovely blond hair down to her waist, and because she was too much afraid of my father.

Usually on these holidays in the mountains my grandmother — my father's mother — joined us. She didn't stay with us, but in an hotel in the village. We used to go and see her and would find her under the big sunshade on the little terrace of the hotel. She was small with tiny feet in little black boots with diminutive buttons. She was proud of her little feet peeping out under her skirt, and she was proud of her head of curly white hair, combed into a high bushy helmet. My father took her every day for a 'short stroll'. They went along the main roads as those little boots and small heels could not manage the paths. He walked in front taking long strides, with his hands behind his back, a pipe in his mouth, and she stepping quickly on her tiny heels. She never wanted to go the way she had been the day before; she always wanted a new road. 'This is where we went yesterday,' she would complain. Without turning round my father would reply absently, 'No, it is another one.' But she persisted: 'It is yesterday's road, it is yesterday's road.' Then she would say. 'I have got a cough and I am choking.' But he pushed on ahead without turning round. 'I have got a cough and I am choking,' she would repeat, putting her hand to her throat. She always repeated the same things two or three times. She would say, 'That wretch Fantecchi that made me have my dress made in brown. I wanted it blue.' And she jabbed her umbrella at the ground with fury. My father took her to watch the sunset over the mountains. But she went on jabbing her umbrella at the ground in a temper, shaking with anger at Fantecchi, her dressmaker. Anyway she only came to the mountains in order to be with us. She lived in Florence for the rest of the year, and we in Turin, and so we only saw one another in the summer. But she could not stand mountains, and her dream would have been to go on holiday to Fiuggi or Salsomaggiore, where she had spent the summers of her youth.

In the past my grandmother had been very well-off, but she had been impoverished by the First World War. This was because she could not believe that Italy could win and believed blindly in the Emperor Franz-Josef. She insisted on holding on to some Austrian investments and so had lost a large amount of money. My father, an irredentist, had vainly tried to persuade her to sell those Austrian investments. My grandmother would refer to this loss of money as 'my misfortune' and would be in despair about it most mornings, pacing up and down the room and wringing her hands. But really she was not as poor as all that. Her beautiful house in Florence was full of Indian and Chinese furniture and Turkish carpets. Her grandfather, Parente, had been a collector of works of art. Portraits of her various forebears hung on the walls. There was grandfather Parente and 'La Vendée', an aunt who was so called because she was a reactionary and kept a salon for diehards and reactionaries. There were many aunts and cousins who were all named either Margherita or Regina, names common in Jewish families in the past. Among those portraits, however, there was not one of my grandmother's father, and one was not allowed to speak of him. The reason was that he had been left a widower, and after a quarrel one day with his two daughters, who were already grown up, he had, in order to spite them, declared that he would marry the first woman he met in the street, and that is what he had done; or that was the story in the family. I do not know if in truth she was the first woman he had encountered as he went out of the front door. At any rate, by this second wife he had had another daughter whom my grandmother refused to know about, and always

13

referred to with disgust as 'Papa's baby'. On our summer holidays we used occasionally to meet 'Papa's baby', by now a mature lady in her fifties. My father would say to my mother: 'Did you see Papa's baby girl? That was Papa's baby!'

'You make a shambles of the whole place. This whole house is a shambles,' my grandmother kept saying, meaning that to us nothing was sacred. It became a famous saying in the family, and was used whenever we found ourselves laughing about someone who was dead, or a funeral. My grandmother had a profound aversion to animals, and went crazy when she saw us playing with a cat, saying we were bound to catch a disease and pass it on to her. 'That horrible little beast,' she would say, stamping her feet and jabbing her umbrella at the ground. She hated them all, and was terrified of disease, but she was, in fact, very healthy, and she was over eighty when she died without ever needing either a doctor or a dentist. She was constantly afraid that one of us would christen her out of spite, because on one occasion one of my brothers as a joke had made the baptismal sign. Every day she said her prayers in Hebrew, without understanding a word, since she did not know the language. She shuddered at people who were not Jews, as she did at cats. My mother was the only exception. She was the only non-Jewish person in all her life for whom my grandmother had any affection. My mother was fond of her and used to say that for all her selfishness she was as innocent and simple as a baby at the breast. By her own account as a young woman my grandmother had been the second most beautiful girl in Pisa, the first having been her friend Virginia del Vecchio. A certain Signore Segrè came to Pisa and asked to be introduced to the most beautiful girl there, to ask for her hand in marriage. Virginia did not accept him. So they introduced him to my grandmother. But she refused him as well, saying that she would not take 'Virginia's leavings'.

She married my grandfather Michele, the kindest and gentlest of men. She was widowed at an early age, and once we asked her why she had not married again. She answered with a harsh laugh and a brutal frankness that we would never have expected of that old lady, querulous and complaining as she was. 'None of that now! Have him pocket everything I have?'

On these mountain holidays my mother, my brother and my sister sometimes complained of boredom in those isolated houses where they had no distractions or company. Being the youngest I could amuse myself with very little and I did not yet feel the boredom of the holidays.

My father would say, 'You lot get bored because you have no inner life.'

One year we were particularly short of money, and it looked as though we should have to spend the summer in the city. However, at the last moment a house was found at a low cost, in a village known as Saint-Jacques d'Ajas. The house had no electric light, only oil lamps. It must have been very small and inconvenient since throughout the summer my mother did nothing but say, 'What a bitch of a house! What a hole Saint-Jacques d'Ajas is!' Our only resource was some books, eight or ten leather-bound numbers of some weekly periodical with games, puzzles and hair-raising thrillers. They had been lent to my brother Alberto by his friend Frinco. We survived on Frinco's books the whole summer. Then my mother made friends with a lady in the house next door. They got talking while my father was not around. He said it was a *negrigura* talk to one's neighbours. But as it turned out later that this Signora Ghiran lived in Turin, in the same building as Frances and knew her by sight, it was possible to introduce her to my father, who was very polite. The truth was that my father was diffident and suspicious of strangers, being afraid they might be 'questionable characters'. But as soon as he discovered some sort of acquaintance in common he was reassured.

My mother did nothing but talk of Signora Ghiran, and at meals we had dishes which Signora Ghiran had told us about, 'A new star rising,' my father said every time this lady was mentioned. 'A new star rising', or simply 'rising star' was his sarcastic greeting for all our new fads.

'I don't know how we should have managed without Frinco's books and Signora Ghiran,' my mother said at the end of that summer.

Our return to the city was marked by the following episode. After a couple of hours in the mail-coach we arrived at the station and took our places in the train. Suddenly we realized that our luggage had been left on the platform. The guard raised his flag and shouted 'Away she goes.' 'Oh no she doesn't,' my father roared with a shout

15

that echoed through the whole coach, and the train did not move until the last of our bags was on board.

Back in town we had, sadly, to part with Frinco's books as he wanted them back, and as for Signora Ghiran we never saw her again. 'You ought to invite Signora Ghiran,' my father said occasionally. 'It is rude not to do so.'

But my mother was extremely capricious and unstable in her relationships. Either she saw people every day, or she had no wish ever to see them again. She was incapable of cultivating acquaintances purely out of politeness. She was always afraid she would get 'fed up' with them, and was afraid that people would come and call when she wanted to go out.

The friends that my mother did see were always the same ones. Apart from Frances, and a few other ladies who were married to my father's friends, my mother always chose friends quite a bit younger than herself; newly married, rather badly off young women to whom she could give advice, and recommend little dressmakers. She hated 'old girls', as she called them, meaning women who were much the same age as herself. She hated entertaining. If one of her old acquaintances wrote to say that she was coming to see her, she panicked. 'Then I shall not be able to go for a walk today,' she would say despairingly. Her young friends, on the other hand, she could take along for a walk or to the cinema. They were easy and at her compliant disposal and prepared to keep up an informal relationship with her. And if they had babies, so much the better; she was very fond of babies. Sometimes in the afternoon all these friends would come to call together. They were known in my father's language as 'the babas'. When supper-time was approaching, he would shout from his study, 'Lydia, Lydia! Have all those "babas" gone?' And the last 'baba' could be seen slinking in terror down the passage and slipping out through the front door. All my mother's young friends were extremely frightened of my father. At supper he would say to my mother, 'Aren't you fed up with "babaing"? Aren't you fed up with their prattling?'

Occasionally my father's friends came to the house for the evening. Like him they were university lecturers, biologists and scientists. On these evenings my father would ask at supper, 'Have you prepared some refreshments?' Refreshments meant tea and biscuits. Nothing

16

stronger ever entered our house. Sometimes my mother had not prepared anything, so my father lost his temper: 'What do you mean by no refreshments? You can't have people in without refreshments. We can't have *negrigure*.'

Among my parents' most intimate friends were the Lopezes — Frances and her husband — and the Ternis. Frances's husband's name was Amadeo but he had been nicknamed 'Lopez' from the days when he and my father were students together. As a student my father had been nicknamed 'Pom' — for *pomodoro*, a tomato — because of his red hair. But if anybody called him 'Pom' he got very angry. He only allowed my mother to call him that. However, when the Lopezes referred among themselves to our family they spoke of 'the Poms' just as we in the same way called them 'the Lopezes'. No one has ever been able to explain to me why Amadeo had this nickname, and I think the reason was lost in the mists of time. Amadeo was stout and had white curly hair, as fine as silk; he rolled his 'r's as did his wife and their three boys, who were our friends. The Lopezes were much smarter and more up-to-date than we were; they had a better apartment, including a lift, and a telephone, which hardly anyone had in those days. Frances often went to Paris and brought back the latest things in clothes and other fashions. One year she returned with a Chinese game in a box decorated with dragons. It was called Mah-Jong. The Lopezes had all learnt to play this Mah-Jong and Lucio, their youngest son, who was my age, was always bragging about Mah-Jong; but he would never teach me how to play it. He said it was too complicated, and that his mother would not allow the box to be touched. I was torn with envy when I saw this forbidden box, so full of mystery, at their house.

When my parents went to the Lopezes for an evening, on their return my father said wonderful things about their house, the furniture and the tea which was served on a trolley in beautiful porcelain cups. He would say that Frances knew 'how to get on'; that is she knew where to find nice furniture and nice cups, she understood furnishing a house, and how tea should be served.

We could not quite make out whether the Lopezes were richer or poorer than us. My mother maintained that they were much richer, but my father said no, they were like us without so very much money — it was only that Frances knew how 'to get on' and was not 'a

17

blockhead, like you lot'. All the same my father considered himself very poor, especially in the early morning when he woke up. He would wake my mother and say, 'I don't know how we are going to carry on any longer.' 'Have you noticed that the Property shares have gone down?' The Property shares were always going down; they never went up. 'Those blasted Property shares,' my mother would say, and complained that my father had no business sense, and that as soon as a worthless share was available he promptly bought some. She often begged him to go to a stockbroker for advice. That made him furious, because in this as in everything else he wanted to do things his own way.

As for the Ternis, they were very rich. Nevertheless, Terni's wife, Mary, was a woman of simple tastes and saw few people. She spent her days just watching her two young children, with their nanny, Assunta, who was dressed entirely in white. Both Mary and the nanny, who imitated her, sat whispering ecstatically 'ssst! ssst!' Even Terni always went 'ssst! ssst!' when he was watching his children, in fact he went 'ssst! ssst!' about everything — our maid Natalina who was anything but beautiful, or some old dresses which he saw mother and my sister wearing. He said of every woman he saw that she had 'an interesting face' and resembled some famous picture. He would stand looking at her for a few minutes, and get out his monocle and polish it on a very fine white handkerchief.

Terni was a biologist and my father had a very high opinion of his work. But he used to say 'that simpleton Terni' because he considered that in his personal life he was a *poseur*. Every time he met Terni he would come back and say 'Terni's a *poseur*', and a moment later again, 'I think he is a *poseur*.' When Terni came to see us he would as a rule stop in the garden and talk with us about novels. He was a cultivated man and had read all the modern novels and was the first to bring *A la recherche du temps perdu* into our house. In fact when I think about it now, I believe that he was trying to model himself on Swann. There was that monocle and his way of discovering in each of us a resemblance to some famous picture. My father would roar to him from his study to come and discuss tissue cells: 'Terni, come here! Don't be such a silly man!' 'Don't be such a clown!' he yelled, when Terni with his little ecstatic whispers poked his nose into the dusty old dining-room curtains and asked if they were new.

THE things that my father appreciated and admired were: Socialism, England, Zola's novels, the Rockefeller Foundation, mountains, and the guides in the Val d'Aosta. The things that my mother liked: Socialism, Paul Verlaine's poems, and music, particularly *Lohengrin*, which she used to sing to us, in the evenings after supper.

My mother was Milanese but she was originally from Trieste as well, and with my father she had married a lot of Triestine expressions. Milanese dialect reappeared when she talked about childhood memories.

Once when she was little, walking down the street in Milan she had seen a big-chested man standing motionless in front of a hairdresser's window, gazing at one of the wax heads and saying under his breath: 'Lovely, lovely. Too long in the neck.'

Many of her memories were like that — simple phrases that she had heard. One day she was out for a walk with her schoolmates and the mistresses. Suddenly one of the little girls broke from the crocodile and running to embrace a dog passing by, she flung her arms round it and cried: 'She . . ., she . . ., she's my little dog's sister!'

My mother was at boarding-school for many years, and had much enjoyed it. She had acted, sung and danced in school entertainments; she had sung in a light opera called *The Slipper in the Snow*.

She had written an opera and set it to music. Her opera began like this:

> I am Don Carlos Tadrid
> I am a student in Madrid
> One fine morning that I'd been a-
> Strolling through the Berzuellina
> At a window I beheld
> A girl all other girls excelled.

And she had written a poem which went thus:

> Fair Ignorance our homage take!
> At thought of thee is quelled my stomach-ache!
> Health reigns where e'er thy presence is,

19

Leave learning to the Maccabbees!
Come, drink and dance, think never a thought
Let us celebrate!
Come, Muse, inspire,
Dictate to me what my heart says
Say the philosopher is a bore,
And love among the ignorant has his part.

And then she had written a parody of Metastasio:

If every fellow's secret vow
Were plain to read upon his brow,
Then no one more on foot would fare,
But ride abroad in chaise and pair.

She had stayed at boarding-school until she was sixteen. On Sundays she used to go to see a maternal uncle called 'Whiskers'. There would be turkey for dinner. After they had eaten, Whiskers would point to the remains of the turkey and say to his wife, 'You and me'll eat that lot tomorrow morning.'

Aunt Celestina, Whiskers' wife, was called 'Baryte'. Someone had explained to her that there was baryte in everything. So she would point at the bread on the table for instance, and say: 'You see that bread there? It is all baryte.'

Whiskers was a crude man and had a red nose. My mother used to say 'a nose like Whiskers' ' when she saw a red one. After those turkey dinners he would say to her: 'Lydia, you and me knows about chemistry, what does sulphuric acid pong of? Pongs of fart. Sulphuric acid pongs of fart.'

Whiskers' real name was Perego. Some friends had made up this couplet: 'By day and night we have a merry go / At the house and cellar of our Perego.'

His sisters, being very devout, were known to us as 'Le Beate', the blessed women.

My mother had another aunt, Aunt Cecilia, who was famous for the following saying. My mother had once told her that they had been anxious about my grandfather who was very late in coming home; they were afraid that something had happened to him. Aunt Cecilia suddenly asked: 'And what did you have for lunch, rice or *pasta*?'

'*Pasta*,' said my mother.

20

'A good thing you did not have rice, or who knows how long he would have been.'

My maternal grandparents both died before I was born. My grandmother, Granny Pina, came from a humble family. She and my grandfather were neighbours in the same block of flats. He wore spectacles and was a rising young advocate, and she used to hear him ask the concierge every day: 'Are there any "laters" for me?' That was how he pronounced 'letters' and my grandmother thought this a mark of distinction. She married him for that and because she wished to have a black velvet coat for the winter. It was not a happy marriage.

As a young woman Grandmother Pina was a charming blonde. She had once acted in an amateur dramatic show. As the curtain rose she was on stage with a brush and an easel and had the following lines: 'I cannot go on painting. My soul will not bend to work and to art. It flies far hence and feeds upon sorrowful thoughts.'

My grandfather plunged into Socialism. He was a friend of Bissolati,[1] Turati[2] and Madame Kulischov.[3] Granny Pina kept aloof from her husband's political life. As he filled the house with Socialists, she used to say with some bitterness about her daughter, 'That girl of ours will be marrying a gas-fitter.'

They ended living apart. In the last years of his life, my grandfather abandoned politics, and resumed practice as a lawyer, but he used to sleep until five in the afternoon and when clients came, he would say, 'What have they come for? Send them away!'

In her last years Granny Pina lived in Florence, and went occasionally to see my mother, who had married meanwhile and was also living in Florence. But Granny Pina was very afraid of my father. She came one day to see my brother Gino, in swaddling clothes, who had a slight temperature. To calm my father who was worried she told him that it might be because he was teething. My father was furious because he maintained that teething could not produce a temperature. As she was leaving she met my Uncle Silvio, who was coming to see us, and whispered on the stairs, 'Don't say it's the teeth,'

Apart from 'Don't say it's the teeth', 'That girl of ours will be marrying a gas-fitter' and 'I cannot go on painting', I know nothing about this grandmother, and no other words of hers have come down

21

to me. That is, I do remember this phrase of hers still used to be quoted in our house: 'Something every day. Something every day. Now Drusilla's bust her specs.'

She had had three children — Uncle Silvio, my mother, and Drusilla who was short-sighted and was always breaking her spectacles. Granny Pina died in Florence in solitude after a life of sorrows. Her eldest child, Silvio, killed himself when he was thirty, blowing his brains out one night in the Milan public gardens.

After her schooldays my mother left Milan and went to live in Florence. She started in the medical faculty there but never finished the course because she met my father and married him. My father's mother was against this marriage because my mother was not Jewish; and someone had told her that my mother was a devout Catholic, and every time she saw a church she crossed herself vigorously. That was not true. No one in my mother's family either went to church or crossed themselves. So for a while my grandmother was opposed to the marriage, but finally she agreed to make my mother's acquaintance. They met at the theatre one evening, at the performance of a play in which there was a white woman who had ended up among the blacks. A black woman who was jealous of her gnashed her teeth and with flaming eyes cried 'White Lady Cutlet, White Lady Cutlet'. Every time my mother ate a chop she said 'White Lady Cutlet'. They had been given complimentary tickets for the stalls at this play, because my father's brother, my uncle Cesare, was a drama critic. This uncle was calm, plump, and always good-humoured — quite different from my father — and as a critic not at all severe. He would never attack a play but always found something good in it. If my mother said she thought a play seemed stupid he got cross and said, 'You just try to write a play like that yourself.' Cesare later married an actress and this was a great tragedy for my grandmother, and for many years she would not let my uncle introduce his wife to her, because to her an actress seemed worse than a woman who crossed herself.

At the time of his marriage my father was working in Florence at the clinic of an uncle of my mother's, who was nicknamed 'the Nutcase' because he was a mental specialist. The Nutcase was in truth a man of great intelligence, cultivated and witty. I do not know if he was ever aware of the family's nickname for him.

22

In my paternal grandmother's house my mother met her varied court of Margheritas and Reginas, my father's cousins and aunts, and also the famous La Vendée who was still alive then. As for my grandfather Parente, he had died a long time before, as had his wife Dolcetta too, and their servant Bepo. Grandmother Dolcetta had been small and round like a ball, and always had indigestion because she ate too much. She would feel unwell, be sick and take to her bed. Then after a while she would be found eating an egg. 'It's fresh,' she would say by way of excuse.

Grandfather Parente and Grandmother Dolcetta had a daughter called Rosina whose husband died leaving her with small children and not much money. So she returned to her father's house. The day after she was home again, while they were all at table Grandmother Dolcetta looked at her and said, 'What is the matter today with our Rosina? She is not her usual self.'

It was my mother who used to tell these stories of Grandmother Dolcetta's egg and of 'our Rosina', because my father told them badly and made a mess of them by breaking in with thunderous snorts of laughter.

My mother on the other hand enjoyed telling stories — story-telling made her happy. Turning to one or other of us at table she would begin a story. Whether it was about my father's family or her own, she became radiant with pleasure, and it always seemed as if she were telling that story for the first time to ears that had never heard it. 'I had an uncle,' she would begin, 'whom everyone called Whiskers.' If one of us said, 'I know that story, I have heard it heaps of times' she would turn to another of us and go on with the story in a low voice. 'I have heard this story so many times,' my father would bellow if he caught what she was saying. My mother would continue under her breath: 'The Nutcase had a lunatic in his clinic who believed he was God. Every day the lunatic said to him. "Good morning, my good Signor Lipmann, good morning", and then the lunatic went on, "Good, perhaps right, Lipmann, probably wrong".'

Then there was the famous saying of a conductor friend of Silvio's who was at Bergamo on tour and said to the singers who were undisciplined or not paying attention: 'We did not come to Bergamo for a picnic but to perform *Carmen,* Bizet's masterpiece.'

There are five of us children. We live in different cities now, some of us abroad, and we do not write to one another much. When we meet we can be indifferent and aloof. But one word, one phrase is enough, one of those ancient phrases, heard and repeated an infinite number of times in our childhood. We have only to say, 'We did not come to Bergamo for a picnic,' or 'What does sulphuric acid pong of?' for us to pick up in a moment our old intimacy and our childhood and youth, linked indissolubly with these words and phrases. One of them would make us recognize each other, in the darkness of a cave or among a million people. These phrases are our Latin, the vocabulary of our days gone by, our Egyptian hieroglyphics or Babylonian symbols. They are the evidence of a vital nucleus which has ceased to exist, but which survives in its texts salvaged from the fury of the waters and the corrosion of time. These phrases are the foundation of our family unity which will persist as long as we are in this world and which is recreated in the most diverse places on earth when one of us says, 'My good Signor Lipmann', and suddenly my father's impatient voice rings in our ears, 'That's enough of that story! I have heard it time and again.'

HOW that stock of bankers who were the forebears and relations of my father ever produced my father and my uncle Cesare, men completely destitute of any business sense, is beyond my comprehension. My father spent his life in scientific research, a profession which never brought him in a penny; his idea of money was as vague and confused as could be, and dominated by basic indifference. So when he happened to have to deal with money, he always lost it, or at least behaved in such a way that he ought to have lost it; and if he did not lose and things went smoothly, it was pure accident. Throughout his life he was dogged by the presentiment that some time or other he would find himself on the street. It was a quite irrational fear which hung around him like his other dark moods and pessimism, like his despair about his children's lack of success, which weighed on him like a mass of black cloud on a mountain top. But in the depths of his heart it never affected his absolutely fundamental inner indifference to money. He would speak of 'a large sum of money' when referring to fifty lire, or as he called it, fifty francs, his monetary unit being the franc and not the lira. In the evenings he would go round the rooms yelling at us for leaving the lights on. But then he could go and lose millions almost without noticing, either with shares which he bought and sold haphazardly, or with publishers to whom he made over his work without troubling to ask for a fair reward.

When my father was made professor at Sassari my parents left Florence and went to live in Sardinia. They lived there for some years and then moved to Palermo where I was born, the youngest of the five children. My father went to the 1915–18 war as a medical officer on the Carso. Finally we came to live in Turin.

Those first years in Turin were difficult ones for my mother. The First World War was scarcely over, there was the post-war period with the high cost of living, and we had little money. It was cold in Turin, and my mother complained of the cold and of the house which my father had taken before our arrival without consulting anybody, which was dark and damp. According to my father, my mother had complained in Palermo, and had complained in Sassari; she had always found something to grumble at. Now she spoke of them as of an earthly paradise. In Sassari and in Palermo she had had a lot of friends, yet she never wrote to them later because she was incapable of keeping in touch with people at a distance.

There she had had lovely houses full of sun, a convenient and easy life and splendid maids. In Turin, to begin with, she could not get maids at all. Finally one day, I don't know how, Natalina arrived in our house, and she stayed for thirty years.

The truth was that although my mother grumbled and complained in Sassari and Palermo, she had been very happy there, because she was cheerful and found people to like and who liked her, and everywhere she found ways of being amused by her surroundings and of being happy. She was even happy in those first years in Turin, years of inconvenience if not actual hardship, in which she often shed tears, because of my father's bad moods, because of the cold, and because of her nostalgia for the places she had left, and because her children were growing bigger and needed books and overcoats and shoes, and there wasn't very much money. All the same she was happy. She was naturally cheerful and scarcely had she stopped crying than she would sing at the top of her voice through the house 'Don Carlos Tadrid' and snatches from *Lohengrin* and *The Slipper in the Snow*. Later when looking back on those years, when she had all the children at home, and there was no money, and the Property shares were always going down, and the house was dark and damp, she always spoke of them as the loveliest and happiest years — 'Via Pastrengo days' she would say to specify the period. (Via Pastrengo is a street we lived in then.)

The house in Via Pastrengo was very large. There were ten or twelve rooms, a courtyard, a garden and a glassed-in veranda which looked on to the garden. It was, however, very dark and certainly damp; one winter two or three toadstools grew in the lavatory. There was a lot of talk in the family about these toadstools and my brothers told my paternal grandmother who was staying with us at the time that we were going to cook and eat them. My grandmother did not believe this but was all the same alarmed and disgusted and said, 'This whole house is a shambles.'

I was a very little girl at that time and had only a vague recollection of Palermo, where I had been born, which I had left when I was three. Yet I liked to think that I too missed Palermo, like my mother and sister, and the beach at Mondello where we used to bathe, a Signora Messina, a friend of my mother's, and a little girl called Olga, a friend of my sister's whom I called 'Live Olga' to distinguish her from my doll of the same name. Every time we saw her on the beach I used to say 'Live Olga makes me shy.' These were the people that were at Palermo and Mondello.

Later, round the table, cradling myself in nostalgia, or with just pretended nostalgia, I composed my first poem:

> Palermino Palermino
> You are nicer than Torino

This effort was hailed in the family as a sign of an early vocation for poetry. Encouraged by my success I immediately wrote two more nonsense rhymes concerning the mountains which I had heard of from my brothers:

Viva La Grivola	Long live La Grivola
Se mai si scivola	If ever we slither,
Viva Il Monte Bianco	Long live Mont Blanc
Se mai sei stanco.	If you are weary.

The habit of writing poems was common in our house. My brother Mario had written one about some boys called Tosi who played with him at Mondello and whom he could not bear:

> Nothing in the world annoys
> Or plagues us like the Tosi boys.

But the most famous and best poem was the one composed by my brother Alberto when he was ten or eleven. This was not based on any reality but created out of nothing, the pure fruit of poetical invention:

> The old spin,
> So flat and thin,
> Has got a baby
> As sweet as may be.

We used to perform d'Annunzio's famous tragedy, *La figlia di*

Jorio. But above all, at home in the evening, we used to recite a poem which my mother had taught us, having heard it as a child at a charity concert in aid of people made homeless by floods in the Po valley.

Gazing in terror day by day they stood.
The old said, 'Oh Madonna, see the flood
Is rising every hour.
Be wise my sons, depart with all your stuff.'
'What! Leave the poor old folk to die alone!'
Daddy would not. But Daddy was young and
    brave and would not believe
So horrible a thing could come to pass.
That night he said to Mummy, 'Now put the babies
To bed, and sleep yourself in peace
The Po is tranquil like a giant at ease
In the earth bed the Lord God for him delves.
Sleep! There are guardian angels and ourselves
Watching upon the banks. Each stalwart arm
Will shield this humble valley from all harm.

My mother had forgotten the rest, and I think she had not remembered these first lines very accurately, because, for one thing where she says, 'Daddy was young and brave', the verse runs on regardless of the metre. But she made good the deficiencies of her memory by the emphasis which she laid on the words: 'Each stalwart arm / Will shield this humble valley from all harm.'

My father could not bear this poem, and when he heard us recite it with our mother, he lost his temper and said we were playing 'theatres' and were incapable of serious matters.

The Ternis came to see us almost every evening, and also some friends of my eldest brother Gino, who was then attending the Polytechnic.

We would all sit round the table and recite poems and sing. 'I am Don Carlos Tadrid, I am a student in Madrid . . .' my mother would sing, and my father, who was reading in his study, would look in at the door of the dining-room every now and then frowning and looking suspicious, with his pipe in his hand, and say: 'Still talking rubbish, still playing theatres!'

The only subjects which he tolerated were scientific subjects, politics and new appointments in the Faculty: as when some professor was brought to Turin, in his opinion wrongly, because he was a silly man, or another was not appointed, wrongly, because he was, in his opinion, 'a very valuable man'. None of us was qualified to follow his talk about scientific subjects or what was going on in the Faculty. But every day at meals he informed my mother either about events in the Faculty, or of what had happened in his laboratory to tissue cultures he had under glass, and he lost his temper if she did not pay attention. He ate a great deal at dinner, but with such speed that he seemed to have eaten nothing, as his plate was empty straight away. He was convinced that he ate little and had imparted this conviction to my mother who was always begging him to eat. He on the other hand would scold her because he considered she ate too much. 'Don't over-eat. You will give yourself indigestion.' 'Don't pick your cuticles,' he roared from time to time. My mother did have this vice of picking her cuticles. She had had it from childhood, when she had had a whitlow at school and the finger had peeled in consequence.

According to my father we all ate too much and would have indigestion. Dishes he did not like he would say were badly made and lay on his stomach. Those he did like he said were good for you and 'stimulated peristalsis'. If a dish which he did not like was served, he was furious. 'Why do you do meat this way? You know I don't like it.' If something he liked was cooked for him alone he became annoyed just the same. 'I don't want special things. Don't make special things for me. I eat anything, I am not difficult like you lot. It is sufficient for me just to eat.'

'One should not talk about eating all the time, it's vulgar,' he bellowed if he heard us discussing one of the courses.

'I do like cheese so much!' my mother never failed to remark every time the cheese was brought in, and my father would say, 'You are monotonous! You do nothing but repeat the same things all the time.'

My father liked fruit very ripe. So if we had a pear which was going bad we gave it to him. 'Ah, you give me your rotten pears, you really are asses,' he would say with a snorting laugh which echoed round the house, and he would eat the pear in two mouthfuls.

'Nuts,' he would say as he cracked them, 'are good for you. They stimulate peristalsis.'

'You are just as monotonous,' my mother would say. 'You repeat the same things all the time, just as you say that I do.'

My father was offended at that and would say, 'You ass! You say I am monotonous. You really are an ass.'

As for politics, we had ferocious arguments which ended in furious scenes, with napkins tossed in the air and doors slammed with enough violence to deafen the whole house. Those were the first years of Fascism. I simply cannot explain why my father and my brothers argued about it so ferociously considering that I believe they were all against Fascism. In recent years I have asked my brothers about it, but none of them can enlighten me; yet they all remembered those ferocious disputes. I think my brother Mario, just to annoy my parents, would defend Mussolini in some fashion, and of course that sent my father into a raging fury. He argued with Mario about everything, because he always found he had the opposite opinion.

My father said of Turati that he was ingenuous, and my mother, who did not think there was anything wrong with ingenuousness, would nod and sigh and say 'My poor Filippetto.' Turati came once to our house when he was passing through Turin, and I remember him in our sitting-room, as big as a bear, with a grey goatee beard. I saw him twice on that occasion, and again later on when he had to escape from Italy, and spent a week with us in hiding. However, I cannot remember a single word he said on that day in our sitting-room; I just remember a lot of yelling and arguing.

My father always came home furious when he had encountered processions of Blackshirts in the street, or when at Faculty meetings he had discovered new Fascists among his acquaintances. 'Clowns, impostors, buffoonery!' he would say as he sat down to dinner, and banged his napkin down, banged his plate down, banged his glass down, and snorted with disgust. He would express his opinions out loud in the street to friends walking home with him and they would look round in terror.

'Cowards! Negroes!' my father would roar when he got in and described their fear, and I think he enjoyed frightening them by talking aloud in the street; partly he enjoyed it, and partly he was unable to control his voice level, which was always very loud, even when he believed he was whispering.

Apropos his inability to control his voice level Terni and my mother used to describe how on one occasion at some professorial function when they were all assembled at the university, my mother asked him in a whisper the name of someone who was standing a few feet away. 'Who is he?' roared my father at his loudest so that everybody turned round. 'Who is he? I can tell you who he is. He is a perfect imbecile.'

My father could not put up with the funny stories which my mother and the rest of us used to tell. We called them 'little jokes' and we had great fun telling them and hearing them. But my father got cross. The only little jokes he could tolerate were those against Fascism or jokes from his day which he knew and my mother knew; he sometimes brought them out in the evening with the Lopezes who had known them for years as well. Some of these little jokes he thought were quite salacious, although I am sure they were quite innocent. When we were present he insisted on telling them in a whisper. His voice then became a sort of noisy buzz in which we could quite easily pick up a lot of words, among them the word *cocotte* which came into all these rather Victorian jokes, and which in his efforts to whisper it, he pronounced louder than any other word and with a particular gusto.

My father always got up at four in the morning. His first thought on waking was to go and see if the *mezzorado* had turned out well. *Mezzorado* was a kind of sour milk which he had learned how to make from some shepherds in Sardinia. It was in fact just yoghurt. In those days yoghurt was not yet the fashion. It was not sold as it is nowadays, in dairies and bars. In eating yoghurt, as in many other things, my father was a pioneer. At that time winter sports were not yet in vogue, and my father was perhaps the only person in Turin to do them. As soon as a little snow had fallen he would be off to Clavières on Saturday evening with his skis on his back. In those days Sestrières did not exist, nor the hotels at Cervinia. As a rule he slept in a refuge above Clavières known as the 'Capanna Mautino'. Sometimes he would take my brothers with him, and some of his assistants who like himself had a passion for the mountains. He had learnt to ski as a young man during a stay in Norway. On his return on Sunday evening he always said the snow had been bad. It was always either too wet or too dry. In the same way the *mezzorado* was never as it should be, and always seemed to be too watery or too thick.

'Lydia! The *mezzorado* has not set,' my father bellowed down the passage. The *mezzorado* was in the kitchen, inside a soup-tureen, covered by a plate, and wrapped in a salmon-pink shawl that had belonged at one time to my mother. Sometimes in fact there was only a greenish watery mess with some lumps of marbly white stuff which had to be thrown away. The *mezzorado* was very tricky, and the smallest thing was enough to spoil it. It was enough if the shawl was a bit out of position and allowed a little air to seep in. 'It has not set again today. It is all your Natalina's fault,' my father bellowed from the passage to my mother who was still half-asleep, and answered rather incoherently from her bed. When we went away for our holiday, we had to remember to take with us the 'mother' of the *mezzorado* which was a small cupful, wrapped in paper and tied with string.

'Where is the mother? Have you brought the mother?' my father would ask on the train, rummaging in the rucksack. 'It's not here, it's not here,' he would cry, and sometimes it had actually been forgotten, and it was necessary to start again from scratch, with beer yeast.

My father had a cold shower in the morning. Under the lash of the water he let out a shout like a long roar, then he dressed and swallowed large cupfuls of freezing cold *mezzorado* with several spoonfuls of sugar. He left the house when the streets were still dark and almost deserted. He went out in the fog and cold of those Turin dawns, wearing a large beret which made a sort of peak over his forehead, and a long roomy raincoat which was all pockets and leather buttons. With his hands behind his back and his pipe in his mouth, he walked along lopsidedly with one shoulder higher than the other. There was practically no one in the streets at that hour; yet he managed to bump into the few there were, as he passed, walking with his head down.

There was no one in the laboratory at that hour; except perhaps Conti, his technician. A short little man, quiet and submissive, in a grey overall. He was very fond of my father who was equally fond of him. Occasionally he came to the house when there was a cupboard to be mended, an electric-light bulb to be changed, or the trunks to be tied up. Through being in the laboratory Conti had learnt anatomy and when examinations were on he used sometimes to prompt the men which made my father angry. But later at home he would tell my mother with some satisfaction that Conti knew more anatomy than

32

the students. In the laboratory my father put on a grey overall just like Conti's and yelled up and down the corridors, just as he did in the passage at home.

'I am Don Carlos Tadrid, I am a student in Madrid,' sang my mother while she was getting up and brushing her hair, which was still sopping wet; for like my father, she had a cold shower, and each of them had these rough thorny gloves to rub down with after the shower in order to warm up again.

'I am freezing,' she would say, but quite happily, because she liked cold water. 'I am still quite freezing. Isn't it cold,' and she went off wrapped in her bath-robe, a cup of coffee in her hand, to take a turn in the garden. My brothers and sister were all at school, and there was for the moment a little peace in the house. She sang and shook out her wet hair in the morning air, and then went to the ironing-room to talk things over with Natalina and Rina.

The ironing-room was also known as the 'wardrobe room'. The sewing-machine was there, and Rina spent the day there, sewing. This Rina was a kind of tame dressmaker, but the only things she was any good at were turning overcoats and patching trousers. She could not make a dress. When she was not with us, she was at the Lopezes. Frances and my mother tossed her backwards and forwards between them. She was a tiny little woman, a kind of dwarf. She called our mother 'Signora Maman', and when she met my father in the passage she scurried off like a mouse, because he could not bear her.

'Rina! So Rina's here again today!' he would bellow, 'I cannot stand her. She is a gossip and she's no good at anything either.'

'But the Lopezes are always sending for her, too,' my mother would say by way of justification.

Rina was a person of uncertain moods. When she came to us after a period of absence she was quite amenable and launched out into thousands of jobs. She would plan to remake all our mattresses and pillows, wash the curtains, take the stains out of the carpets with coffee grounds, just as she had seen it done in Frances's house. She soon got fed up, however. She became sulky, and picked quarrels with Lucio and me who were standing by her because she had promised us a walk and sweets. Lucio was Frances's youngest child and came to us almost every day to play.

'Leave me in peace. I have work to do,' Rina would say crossly as she used the sewing-machine. And she quarrelled with Natalina.

'That blasted Rina!' my mother would say on mornings when she failed to appear without letting her know and no one knew where she had got to as Frances had not seen her either. There were the mattresses and pillows all undone thanks to her enterprise, flocks of wool piled up in the wardrobe-room, and carpets on which the coffee grounds had left yellowish streaks. 'That blasted Rina! I won't have her here any more.'

After a few weeks Rina turned up again, all smiles and politeness and full of plans and promises, and my mother immediately forgot her faults, and stood in the wardrobe-room listening to her chatter, while she sewed away with the machine at great speed, pressing the treadle with her minute dwarf's foot, with a felt slipper.

According to my mother Natalina resembled Louis XI. She was small and slender with a long face and hair which was sometimes tidy and smooth and sometimes extravagantly curled. 'Here comes Louis XI,' my mother would say of a morning when she saw Natalina enter the bedroom, looking rather grim, a scarf round her neck, and a pail and scrubbing-brush in her hand. Natalina used to confuse the personal pronouns. She would say, 'She has gone out this morning without an overcoat.' 'And who is she?' 'Master Mario.' 'They should tell him.' 'Who is they?' 'They? I mean you, Signora Lydia,' Natalina would say with annoyance, banging her pail.

My mother would describe Natalina to her friends as a 'thunderbolt' because of the extraordinary speed with which she got through the housework, or she was an 'earthquake' because she did everything with noise and violence. She had had an unhappy childhood and consequently looked like a whipped dog. She was an orphan and had grown up in orphanages and institutions and then she went into service with unkind mistresses. She looked back on those old mistresses with a sort of regret even though they had boxed her ears enough to make her head ache for days. At Christmas she would send them expensive gilded cards. Sometimes too she sent them presents. She never had a penny in her pocket for she was generous and had large ideas of spending, and was always ready to lend money to her friends with whom she went out on Sundays. Although she never lost that look of a whipped dog, she nevertheless imposed her despotic and obstinate will on us and particularly on our mother. They were strongly attached to each other, yet Natalina

34

maintained a surly, sarcastic and by no means servile attitude towards her. 'Just as well they's a lady, as what would they live off, them that's no good at anything?' she would say to my mother.

'Who do you mean by them?'

'Them, I mean you, you!'

AT HOME we lived always with the nightmare of our father's outbursts of fury which exploded unexpectedly and often for the pettiest reason: a pair of shoes that could not be found, a book out of its proper place, or if a light bulb had gone, dinner was slightly late, or some dish a little over-cooked. And then we also lived with the nightmare of quarrels between my brothers Alberto and Mario which broke out equally unexpectedly. We would suddenly hear a noise in their room of chairs being overturned and thumps against the wall followed by wild piercing yells. Alberto and Mario were big now and very strong, and when they set to with their fists they really hurt each other, and emerged with bleeding noses, swollen lips and torn clothes.

'They are murding each other,' my mother would scream, dropping the 'er' in fright. 'Beppino, come here, they are murding each other,' she would scream to my father.

My father's intervention was as violent as all his actions. He flung himself between the two of them locked in violent combat and whacked them all over. I was a little girl then and can recall my terror at these three men fighting savagely. The reasons for these fights were as futile as those which set off my father's temper: a book or a tie, or who was to wash first. On one occasion when Alberto appeared at school with his head bandaged, one of the masters asked what had happened to him. He stood up and said, 'My brother and I were trying to have a bath.'

Of the two Mario was the taller and stronger. His hands were as hard as iron, and when he was angry his frenzy seemed to paralyse his muscles, his tendons and his jaw. As a child he had been rather slight and my father used to take him for walks in the mountains to make him strong, as in fact he did with all of us. Mario had conceived a dumb hatred of the mountains, and as soon as he was free from his father's control he gave up mountaineering altogether. But in those days he still had to go. Like my father he vented his temper sometimes on inanimate objects; sometimes Alberto was not the target for his wrath but some object that would not obey his furious hands. He would go down to the cellar on a Saturday afternoon to look for his skis. In the course of searching for them he would become possessed by silent fury, either because he could not find the skis or because he could not undo the straps however much he pulled at them. Alberto and my father were part of his anger although at the time they were nowhere near him — Alberto because he used his things, and my father because he persisted in taking Mario to the mountains although he loathed them, and made him take old skis with rusty buckles. Sometimes he would try on his boots and be unable to pull them on. He would rouse the devil down in the cellar all by himself; and we upstairs would listen to the terrific row. He banged all the skis on the floor, he banged the buckles, the boots, the sealskins, he ripped off cords, turned out drawers, and kicked the chairs, the walls, the table legs. I can remember seeing him one day in the sitting-room sitting peacefully reading a newspaper. Suddenly he was seized with one of his silent rages and began to tear the paper furiously. He gnashed his teeth, stamped on the ground, and tore up the paper. On that occasion neither Alberto nor his father was in any way to blame. The simple fact was that the bells of a neighbouring church had begun to ring and the insistent sound of them exasperated him.

There was an occasion at table when my father had shouted at him, and though it was by no means one of his most terrible displays, Mario had picked up the breadknife and started scratching the back of his hand. Blood streamed out. I remember my mother's terror, shouts and tears, and my father being frightened too and shouting as he applied iodine and sterilized gauze.

After quarrelling and fighting with Alberto, Mario would go around for a few days with 'a face', or with 'the moon', as we used to say. He would come to table looking pale, with swollen eyelids and very, very small eyes. Mario's eyes were always small, long and narrow, like a Chinaman's, but when he had 'the moon' they were reduced to barely visible slits. He would not say a word. He generally had a face because he believed that we sided with Alberto against him, and he thought that he was now too old for his father to have the right to slap him.

'Did you see Mario's face? Did you see the moon he's got?' my father would say to my mother when Mario had hardly left the room. 'What is this moon about? He didn't say a single word. What an ass!'

Then one morning Mario's 'moon' would be gone. He would

37

come into the sitting-room, sit in an armchair, stroke his cheeks with an absorbed smile and his eyes closed, and start saying, '*Il baco del calo del malo*'. It was a little joke that he liked and he repeated it interminably, '*Il baco del calo del malo — Il beco del chelo del melo — Il bico del chilo del milo*.'[4] 'Mario,' shouted his father. 'Don't use bad language!'

'*Il baco del calo del malo*,' Mario began again as soon as his father had gone. He remained chatting with his mother in the sitting-room and with Terni, who was his great friend.

'How sweet Mario is when he is good. He's so nice,' my mother would say. 'He is just like Silvio.'

Silvio was my mother's brother who had killed himself. His death was shrouded in mystery. I know now that he killed himself, but I do not really know why. I believe it was my father particularly who spread this air of mystery about Silvio, because he did not wish us to know that there had been a suicide in the family, and possibly for other reasons which I do not know about. My mother for her part always spoke cheerfully of Silvio, because her happy nature affected everything and she recalled what was good and happy in everything and everybody, and left what was painful or bad in the shade, barely allowing it the briefest sigh from time to time.

Silvio had been a musician and a man of letters. He had set some poems of Paul Verlaine — *Les Feuilles Mortes* and some others as well — to music. He played a little, and badly, and used to hum his tunes, accompanying himself on the piano with one finger. He would say to my mother, 'Listen, silly girl, listen to it, isn't it lovely?'

Although he played so badly and sang with a wisp of a voice, my mother used to say it was wonderful to listen to him. Silvio was very smart, and dressed with great care. Woe betide if his trousers were not well-pressed and the crease not quite straight. He had a lovely walking-stick with an ivory knob. He strolled about Milan with this stick and a straw hat and met his friends to talk about music in cafés. In my mother's stories Silvio was always a happy character, and when I heard the details of what happened to him, it seemed inexplicable. There was a faded portrait of him on my mother's dressing-table, with his straw hat and little twirled moustache, and beside it was another photograph of my ·mother with Anna Kulischov in veils and feathered hats, in the rain.

We had also an unfinished opera by Silvio, his *Peer Gynt*. It consisted of several bundles in cardboard boxes tied up with tape, which lay on the top of a cupboard.

'Silvio was such fun,' my mother always said. 'He was so nice. And *Peer Gynt* was a valuable work.'

My mother always hoped that at least one of her children would become a musician, like Silvio. Her hopes remained unfulfilled because we all proved to be completely deaf to music and when we tried to sing we were utterly out of tune. However, we all tried to sing and when Paola was doing her room in the morning she used to sing, in a feeble cat-like voice, snatches of opera and songs she had picked up from my mother. Sometimes Paola went with my mother to a concert and told everyone she liked music. But my brothers said that was a pretence and it meant nothing to her. As for my brothers and me, we were occasionally taken to concerts and invariably we fell asleep; and if we were taken to an opera we complained about 'all that music which stops you hearing the words'. Once my mother took me to hear *Madame Butterfly*. I had the children's paper *Il Corriere dei Piccoli* with me and read it the whole time, trying to decipher the words by the feeble light from the stage, and stopping my ears with my fingers to avoid hearing the awful noise.

Yet when our mother sang, we all listened open-mouthed. Someone once asked Gino if he knew Wagner's operas. 'Yes, of course,' he replied, 'I have heard my mother sing *Lohengrin*.'

My father not only did not care for music, he hated it; he hated every kind of instrument that produced music, whether it was a pianoforte, an accordion or a drum. There was an occasion immediately after the war, when I was in a restaurant with him in Rome and a woman came in to beg. The waiter went to send her away. My father was furious with the waiter, and shouted, 'I forbid you to throw that poor woman out. Leave her alone.' He gave the woman something, and the waiter was offended and angry and retreated to a corner with his napkin on his arm. The woman then took a guitar from beneath her cloak and began to play. After a short while my father began to show signs of impatience, the ones that he showed at meals. He moved his glass about, the bread, the knives and forks, and flapped his napkin on his knees. Bending over him with her guitar, the woman continued to play, being grateful for his protection, and the guitar produced a long melancholy moan.

Suddenly my father exploded. 'Enough of this music. Go away! I cannot stand people playing music.' But she went on and the waiter stood in his corner, silent and motionless, triumphantly enjoying the scene.

In addition to Silvio's suicide there was another matter at home which was always vaguely veiled in mystery: the fact that Turati and Kulischov lived together, although they were not husband and wife. In this sort of mystery I can see especially my father's prejudices and susceptibilities. By herself my mother would probably not have thought of it. It would have been simpler to lie and to tell us that they were married. But no; instead, they concealed from us, or at least from me, who was still a little girl, the fact that they were living together. As I always heard them mentioned together, I asked why, and whether they were husband and wife, brother and sister, or what. I got a rather confused answer. I could not understand where Kulischov's daughter Andreina,[5] a friend of my mother from childhood, had popped out from, and why she was called Costa; and I could not understand how Andrea Costa[6] came into it; he had been dead for some time, but was still frequently mentioned in connection with those people.

Turati and Kulischov always came into my mother's reminiscences. I knew that they were both alive and were living in Milan (possibly together, or possibly in two different houses) and that they were still involved in politics and carrying on the struggle against Fascism. However, they became mixed up in my imagination with other persons who always came into my mother's reminiscences — her parents, Silvio, the Nutcase, and Whiskers. These people were either dead, or if they were still alive, were part of far-away events in remote times, when my mother had been a little girl and had heard the child say 'my little dog's sister', or 'what does sulphuric acid pong of?' They were people whom one could not see or touch any longer, and even if one could, they were not the same as I had imagined them. Even if they were still living they were contaminated by their association with the dead, with whom they lived in my thoughts. They had acquired the light step of dead people that one cannot catch up with.

'Oh poor Lydia,' my mother would sigh from time to time. She was

40

full of self-pity over her troubles, the scarcity of money, my father's outbursts, Alberto and Mario's endless fighting. Then Alberto would not work at school, and was always going off to play football; our sulking, and Natalina's sulking.

I was sometimes sulky and wilful as well, but I was only a little girl and it did not worry my mother much at the time.

'It is all prickly, it is all prickly,' I would say in the morning when my mother was dressing me and putting on one of those woollen vests which irritated my skin.

'They are very good vests from Neuberg's,' my mother used to say, 'you don't expect me to throw those out, do you?'

My mother bought these vests 'from Neuberg's' and if a vest was one of those, it was bound to be good, soft and could not possibly itch, so vests came from Neuberg's; our overcoats were made by Maccheroni the tailor. Our father dealt with our winter boots, and they were ordered from a bootmaker called 'Signor Castagneri' who had a shop in the Via Saluzzo.

I would come into the dining-room still sulking because of my Neuberg vest, and at the sight of my black, cross looks, my mother would say 'Here comes Maria the storm cloud!'

My mother hated the cold and that was why she bought all those Neuberg vests. She hated the cold, the constant penetrating cold of those winter days, although every morning she had an icy shower, which she liked. 'Oh, it's cold!' she would keep saying as she pulled one pullover on top of another and dragged the sleeves down over her hands. 'Oh, it's cold. I cannot stand it when it's cold,' and she would pull my Neuberg vest down over my hips while I tried to wriggle away. 'All wool, Lydia, all wool,' she would say in imitation of an old school friend. 'Just think, to see you in that lovely warm vest I feel much better.'

She hated heat as well. When it was hot she began to pant and loosen the collar of her dress. 'Oh, how hot it is! I cannot stand it when it is hot,' she would say, and my father would say, 'You are so intolerant! You are all so intolerant!'

When she went away with my father she took with her a quantity of pullovers and other clothes of different weights, and did nothing but take things off and put them back on at the smallest variation of temperature. 'I can never get the right temperature,' she would say and my father would reply, 'You are such a bore being hot and cold! You always manage to complain.'

I never wanted breakfast in the morning. I detested milk, and yoghurt even more. However, my mother knew that when I was at Frances's, and at the Ternis too, for elevenses I drank cupfuls of milk. In fact I drank the milk at the Ternis and at Frances's house with great repugnance; out of obedience and shyness when I was away from home. My mother got it into her head that I liked Frances's milk. So every morning a cup of milk was brought to me, and I regularly refused to touch it. 'But it is from Frances's,' my mother would say. 'It is from Lucio's cow.' She gave me to understand that they had fetched the milk from Frances's, that she and Lucio had their own personal cow, the milk in their house was not bought from the milkman but came every day from their estate in Normandy called Le Grouchet. 'It is milk from Le Grouchet, Lucio's milk,' my mother would repeat. But as I resolutely refused to drink it Natalina finally made me some broth.

Although I was the right age I did not go to school because my father used to say you catch germs at school. For the same reason my brothers and sister had their first lessons at home with governesses. My mother gave me lessons. I could not understand arithmetic, and could never learn my tables. My mother shouted herself hoarse over it. She brought pebbles in from the garden and lined them up on the table; or sometimes she used sweets. We never had sweets at home because my father said they ruined one's teeth; and there was never any chocolate or anything like that since it was forbidden to eat between meals. The only sweets we ever ate, and that was always at meals, were certain fritters called *Smarren* which a German cook had taught us to make. It would seem that they were cheap and we had them so often that we could not bear them. Then there was a sweet which Natalina could make. She called it Gressoney pudding because she had learned to make it when we were at Gressoney in the mountains.

So my mother only bought sweets in order to teach me arithmetic. But arithmetic with pebbles and sweets repelled me even more. In order to learn modern teaching methods my mother subscribed to a teachers' periodical called *I Diritti della Scuola*. I do not know what

42

she may have learned about educational methods, but she found a poem in them which she liked very much and used to recite to my brothers:

> We'll cry in one band,
> 'Long live the gracious hand
> Of the little lady who
> Lives a life of virtue.'

In geography lessons my mother talked about all the countries my father had visited as a young man. He had been to India where he had had cholera and, I believe, yellow fever; he had been to Germany and Holland; he had also been to Spitzbergen. There he had been inside the cranium of a whale to look for the cerebro-spinal ganglia; but he had not been successful. He had been covered all over with whale's blood, and the clothes which he had brought back were crusted and stiff with dried blood. We had a lot of photographs in the house of my father with whales. My mother used to show them to me, but I was rather disappointed since the photographs were out of focus, and my father only appeared in the background as a minute shadow. And you could not see either the head or the tail of the whale, you could only see a kind of fuzzy grey hill with a chasm cut through it; and that was the whale.

Lots of roses grew in our garden in the spring. How they did I cannot say, since none of us ever dreamed of watering them or of pruning the bushes. A gardener came, rather irregularly, once a year, and it seemed that was enough.

'The roses, Lydia, the violets, Lydia,' my mother would say as she went round the garden, mimicking her old school friend. The Terni children used to come to our garden in the spring with their nanny, Assunta, who had a white apron and stockings of white Scotch wool. She took her shoes off and placed them beside her on the grass. The Terni children, Cucco and Lullina, were also dressed in white, and my mother would put my pinafores on them so that they could play without getting dirty. 'Ssst, sst! look what Cucco is doing!' Terni would say, admiring his children playing in the dirt. Terni took off his shoes and jacket on the grass too in order to play ball. But he slipped them on again immediately if he heard my father coming.

We had a cherry-tree in the garden and Alberto used to climb up it and eat cherries with his friends; there was Frinco, the one with the books, a stern figure in a sweater and a peaked cap, and Lucio's brothers.

Lucio came in the morning and left in the evening. In spring and summer he was always at our house, since his parents had no garden. Lucio was a delicate frail youth and never had any appetite at meals. He would eat a little, sigh and put down his fork. 'I am tired of chewing,' he would say, rolling his r's like the rest of his family. Lucio was a Fascist and my brothers made him lose his temper when they were rude about Mussolini. 'Don't let us talk politics,' Lucio would say the moment he saw my brothers coming. As a child he had thick locks of black hair, like long bananas down his forehead. Later these were cut short; and then his hair was tidy and smooth and shone with brilliantine. He was always dressed like a little man, with close-fitting jackets and bow-ties. He had learnt to read with me; but I had read a pile of books, and he very, very few because he read slowly and got tired. However, when he was at our house he read too. For when I was bored with playing I would get a book and fling myself on the grass. Lucio even started boasting to my brothers that he had read a whole book, because they were always chaffing him for reading so little. 'Today I have read two liras. Today I have read five liras,' he would say looking pleased and pointing at the price on the cover. In the evening a maidservant came to collect him: a wrinkled old lady called Maria Buoninsegni, with a worn fox fur round her neck. This Maria Buoninsegni was very devout and took Lucio and me to church and to processions. She was a friend of Father Semeria, and was always talking about him. On one occasion she took us to some service or other and presented us to Father Semeria, who patted our heads and asked us if we were her children. 'No, some friends' children,' replied Maria Buoninsegni.

NEITHER Lopez nor Terni liked mountaineering, so my father occasionally went on his expeditions and climbs with a friend called Galeotti.

Galeotti lived at a place in the country called Pozzuolo, with his sister and a nephew. My mother once went to stay with them there; she enjoyed herself very much. She often talked about those days at Pozzuolo. There were chickens and turkeys and they had huge meals. Galeotti's sister, Adele Rasetti, took my mother for walks and told her the names of herbs and plants and insects, for in that family they were all entomologists and botanists. Adele had also given her one of her pictures, a view of an Alpine lake, which we had hung in our dining-room. Adele got up early to do the accounts with the bailiff. paint, or go out 'botanizing'. She was small and thin, with a sharp nose, and a straw hat. 'Isn't Adele wonderful?' my mother used to say. 'She gets up early, she paints, she botanizes.' She herself could not paint and could not distinguish basil from chicory. My mother was lazy and always full of admiration for energetic people. Every time she saw Adele Rasetti she would start reading scientific manuals in order to learn something about plants and insects, but then she got bored and gave up.

In the summer Galeotti used to visit us in the mountains and bring his nephew, Adèle's son, who was a friend of my brother Gino. My grandmother would pace up and down the room in the morning anxiously wondering what dress to put on. 'Put on that grey one with the little buttons,' said my mother. 'No, Galeotti has already seen it,' she replied, wringing her hands in uncertainty.

Galeotti took little notice of my grandmother, since he was always busy talking to my father and planning walks and climbs. My grandmother did not like Galeotti at all, in spite of her anxiety not to be seen in 'yesterday's dress'. She thought he was uncouth and unsophisticated and was afraid he might take my father to dangerous places.

Galeotti's nephew was called Franco Rasetti. He was a physics student, and he too was mad on collecting insects and minerals. Gino caught this mania too. They returned from expeditions with clumps of moss in their handkerchiefs, dead beetles and crystals in their rucksacks. Franco talked incessantly at meals, and always about physics, geology and beetles, and as he talked he gathered all the crumbs on the table-cloth with his finger. He had a sharp nose and a pointed chin, a rather lizardlike greenish complexion, and a bristling moustache. 'He is very intelligent,' my father said, 'but dry. He is very dry.'

However, despite his dryness Franco had written a poem once on the way back from a hike with Gino, while they were in a deserted hut and waiting for the rain to stop:

> Slow and even falls the rain
> On black rocks and pastures green.
> Vague forms dissolve into the wisps
> Of cloud that veil them in mists.

Gino did not write poems, and in fact did not like either poetry or novels. But he liked this poem very much and he often recited it. It was a long one, but I only remember this one verse.

I too thought that poem about the black rocks very beautiful, and I was green with envy at not having written it myself. It was simple. I myself had seen green pastures and dark rocks so often in the mountains. It had never occurred to me that one could make anything of them. I had looked at them and that was all. So poetry was like that; simple and made from nothing that could be seen. I looked about me attentively for something like those black rocks and pastures green and which this time I would not allow to be taken from me by anyone else.

'Gino and Rasetti are are good walkers,' said my father, 'they have done the Aiguille Noire de Peteré. They are all right. A pity that Rasetti is so dry. He doesn't talk politics. He is not interested. He is as dry as dust.'

'But Adele is not dry, no,' my mother said. 'Isn't she wonderful! She gets up early, she paints. I'd like to be like Adele.'

Galeotti was always cheerful. He was a short rather stout man and wore rough grey tweeds; he had a short white moustache, fair hair turning white and a bronzed face. We were all extremely fond of him. But I don't recall anything else about him.

46

One day Terni and my mother were standing in the hall; my mother was crying. They said that Galeotti was dead.

The words 'Galeotti is dead' remained in my memory always. Until that moment no one during my existence in this world, no one whom we had known so well, had died. Death became indissolubly linked in my mind with that cheerful figure in grey tweeds who so often came to visit us in the mountains during summer.

Galeotti had died unexpectedly of pneumonia. Many years later, after the discovery of penicillin, my father often said: 'If there had been penicillin in poor Galeotti's time, he would not have died. He died of streptococcal pneumonia. That can be cured now with penicillin.'

As soon as anybody died my father immediately added the adjective 'poor' to his name, and was cross with my mother if she did not do the same. This custom of saying 'poor' was vigorously respected in my father's family. When my grandmother spoke of her sister who was dead, she always said 'poor little Regina', and never spoke of her in any other way.

So Galeotti became 'poor Galeotti' barely an hour after his death. The news of his end was conveyed to my grandmother with great caution. She was constantly afraid of dying, and did not like it at all if death came anywhere near her.

After Galeotti's death my father said he no longer really enjoyed climbing. He continued all the same, but without his old enthusiasm. Both he and my mother spoke of the days when they were younger as a happy cheerful time: Galeotti was still alive, the mountains still held a particular fascination for my father, and it seemed that Fascism was bound to come to an end.

'ISN'T Mario sweet? Isn't he nice,' said my mother smoothing Mario's hair when he was hardly out of bed, and his little eyes were almost invisible for sleepiness.

'*Il baco del calo del malo*,' said Mario with an absorbed smile, rubbing his jaw. This was his way of announcing that he was not sulking and would chat with my mother, my sister and me.

'Isn't Mario sweet, isn't he handsome!' said my mother. 'He looks like Silvio, he looks like Suess Aja Cawa!'

Suess Aja Cawa was a well-known film actor at that time. When my mother saw his slanting eyes and bony cheeks on the screen, she would shout, 'That's Mario! It really is!'

'Don't you think that Mario is handsome?' she would ask my father.

'I don't find him all that handsome, Gino is more handsome,' my father would answer.

'Gino is handsome too,' said my mother then. 'Isn't Gino nice. My Ginetto! The one thing I really care about is my sons. I only have fun with my sons.'

When Gino and Mario had new suits from Maccheroni, the tailor. my mother would embrace them and say, 'I like my sons more than ever when they have new suits.'

We used to have heated discussions at home about whether people were handsome or ugly. We would argue about whether a certain Signora Gilda, governess to some friends of ours, was pretty or not. My brothers maintained that she was very ugly and had a kind of dog-like snout, but my mother said that she was extraordinarily beautiful.

'What!' shouted my father with one of his shouts of laughter that echoed through the house, 'Beautiful, that woman?'

And there were continual arguments as to whether the Colombos or the Cohens were uglier. These were friends we met in the mountains in the summer. 'The Cohens are uglier,' my father shouted. 'Do you want to put them with the Colombos? There is no comparison. The Colombos are better. You don't use your eyes. You people don't use your eyes!'

Speaking of his various cousins who were either called Margherita or Regina, my father used to say that they were beautiful. 'As a young woman,' he would begin, 'Regina was very beautiful . . .' 'Oh, no, Beppino,' my mother would say, 'she had a sticking out chin.' She thrust forward her chin and lower lip to show how Regina's jaw stuck out, and my father lost his temper.

'You don't know anything about good or bad looks. You think the Colombos are uglier than the Cohens.'

Gino was serious, quiet and good at school; he did not fight with either of his brothers. He was good at mountaineering, so he was my father's favourite. My father never called him an ass. He used to say, however, that he never 'unwound' in the sense of relaxing. Gino in fact never 'unwound' because he was always reading, and when spoken to answered only in monosyllables without raising his head from his book. When Alberto and Mario were fighting he continued to read without stirring, and my mother had to call him and shake him in order to get him to separate them. While he read he ate bread very very slowly, roll after roll, and would consume a kilo or more after lunch.

'Gino!' my father would cry, 'you never unwind. You never say anything; and you must not eat all that bread, you will give yourself indigestion.' Gino did in fact often have indigestion. He had a red face, flapping ears as red as fire, and a scowl. 'What has Gino got that face for? What is that moon for? You don't think he's got into trouble, do you?' my father would ask my mother, waking her in the night. My father could never tell if his sons were sulking or had indigestion.

When they really had indigestion he suspected dark stories of women, *cocottes* as he called them.

My father used occasionally to take Gino to the Lopezes in the evening since he considered him the steadiest, best behaved and most presentable of his sons. Gino, however, had the failing of going to sleep after meals, and would even drop off in the Lopezes' arm-chair while Frances was talking to him. His eyes became very small, his head nodded gently, and after a moment he was asleep, with a faint happy smile and his hands in his lap.

49

'Gino!' my father shouted. 'Don't go to sleep. You are asleep!'

'You people,' my father would say, 'are not fit to be taken anywhere.'

On one side were Gino and Rasetti, and the mountains, the black rocks, crystals and insects. On the other side were Mario and my sister Paola and Terni, all of whom detested mountaineering and liked stuffy rooms, gloom, and cafés. They liked Casorati's pictures, Pirandello's plays, Verlaine's poetry, Gallimard's publications, Proust. These were two quite separate worlds. I did not know yet which one I would choose. Both attracted me. I had not yet decided whether to spend my life studying beetles, chemistry and botany, or whether I would paint pictures or write novels. In the world of Gino and Rasetti everything was clear, everything happened in daylight, everything was plausible, there were no mysteries or secrets. On the other hand, Terni, Paola and Mario's conversations were rather mysterious and impenetrable in a way which I found both fascinating and bewildering.

'What's Terni got to whisper about with Mario and Paola?' my father asked my mother. 'They are always there whispering in a corner. What is all this rigmarole?'

In my father's terms this meant secrets and he could not bear to see people absorbed in conversation and not know what it was all about.

'They are probably talking about Proust,' my mother told him.

She had read Proust, and she too, like Terni and Paola, liked his work very much. She told my father that this Proust was someone who was very fond of his mother and his grandmother, he had asthma, and could never sleep and as he could not stand noise he had had the walls of his room lined with cork.

'He must have been a cad,' said my father.

My mother had not made a choice between these two worlds, and sometimes lived in one for a while and sometimes in the other, and enjoyed being in both of them, because her curiosity never rejected anything but fed on every kind of food and drink.

My father on the other hand cast a grim suspicious eye upon anything new and unfamiliar, and he was afraid that the books which Terni brought to the house might not be suitable for us. 'Is this suitable for Paola?' he asked my mother as he leafed through *A la recherche*, reading a few words here and there. 'It must be boring stuff,' he added as he threw the book down. And the fact that it was 'boring stuff' reassured him somewhat.

As for the pictures by Casorati[7] that Terni brought us reproductions of, my father could not stand them. 'Daubing dishwater,' he said.

In any case painting did not interest him at all. When they travelled he would accompany my mother to picture galleries, allowing to old masters like Goya or Titian a certain authenticity because they were universally recognized and acclaimed. He insisted, however, on very rapid visits to galleries and would not allow my mother to linger in front of the pictures. 'Come on, Lydia, let us go,' he would say and drag her away. He was always in a hurry when he travelled.

My mother was not very interested in painting either. She knew Casorati personally, however, and liked him. 'What a handsome face he has!' she said, and as she thought he was handsome she liked his pictures too.

'I have been to Casorati's studio,' my sister said on coming home one day.

'Casorati is so nice, and so handsome,' said my mother.

'What the devil is Paola doing going to Casorati's studio?' asked my father with a suspicious frown. He was always afraid that we should get into trouble, that is become entangled in shady love affairs; he saw threats to our chastity everywhere.

'Nothing really. She went with Terni, and they went to see Nella Marchesini,' my mother explained.

Nella Marchesini was a childhood friend of my sister's and my father knew her well and had a good opinion of her; so her name was enough to reassure him. Nella Marchesini was studying painting with Casorati, and so her presence in his studio was quite all right. To be accompanied by Terni, on the other hand, would not have been enough to reassure him, since he did not regard Terni as a reliable chaperone.

'What a lot of time Terni has to waste,' he would say, 'he would do better to finish his work on tissue pathology. It is a year since I heard him talk about it.'

'You know that Casorati is an anti-Fascist?' said my mother. Now anti-Fascists were becoming more and more rare. So my father cheered up when he heard of one.

'Oh, he is an anti-Fascist. Really.' He sounded interested. 'Still, his

51

pictures are a lot of dishwater. How can people possibly like them!'

Terni was a great friend of Petrolini[8] the comedian, and when Petrolini came to Turin to give a series of performances Terni had complimentary tickets for the stalls almost every evening which he gave to my mother and the others.

'How lovely,' said my mother, 'we are going to see Petrolini again this evening. I do love being in the stalls. Petrolini is so nice, and such fun! Silvio would have liked him so much too.'

'So this evening you are abandoning me, are you?'

'But why don't you come too, Beppino?'

'Pooh! Can you see me going to see Petrolini! I couldn't care less about Petrolini! That clown.'

'We went with Terni to see Petrolini in his dressing-room,' my mother said the next day, 'and Mary came too; they are great friends with Petrolini.'

The fact that Terni's wife Mary should be there too was a weighty and reassuring factor in my father's eyes. He had the highest admiration for Mary. Her presence went a long way toward making evenings at the theatre, and even perhaps Petrolini himself, legitimate and respectable. However, he continued to run him down, and imagined that he put on a false nose and bleached his hair to act.

'I cannot understand how Mary can be such a friend of Petrolini. I cannot understand how she can enjoy going to see him. I can understand Terni and you lot. You like silly things so much. But how come they are such friends with him? He must be a doubtful character.'

To my father, an actor, especially a comedian who made faces on the stage in order to get a laugh, was bound to be 'a doubtful character'. My mother, however, reminded him that his brother Cesare had spent his life with actors and had married an actress. It was not possible that those people Cesare knew could all be 'doubtful characters' even if they did come on the stage dressed up, and dyed their hair and moustaches.

'And Molière,' said my mother, 'was not Molière an actor? Are you going to tell me that he was "a doubtful character" then?'

'Ah, Molière,' said my father, who greatly admired Molière, 'Molière is marvellous. Poor Cesare was mad about Molière. But you aren't going to put Molière on a level with Petrolini, are you?' he

52

roared with one of those thunderous snorts of laughter pouring the greatest contempt on Petrolini.

My mother, Paola and Mario generally went to the theatre together, and usually with the Ternis, for whom, if they did not have complimentary tickets for stalls, Petrolini always had a box and invited them. So my father could not say, 'I don't want you throwing your money away on the theatre.' Instead he looked kindly on an evening my mother spent with Mary.

'You are always going out,' he would say to my mother. 'You always leave me behind.'

'But you always shut yourself up in your study,' she would say. 'You never keep me company.'

'What an ass you are! You know that I have a lot to do. I do not have time to waste like the rest of you. Anyway, I did not marry you to keep you company.'

My father worked in his study in the evenings. He corrected the proofs of his books and pasted in illustrations. Occasionally, however, he read a novel. My mother would ask, 'Is it good, your novel, Beppino?' 'Bah! Boring! Silly nonsense!' he would reply with a shrug of his shoulders. But he read very attentively, smoked his pipe and brushed the ash off the pages. When he came home after a journey he always brought with him detective stories which he had bought at the station bookstalls, and finished them in his study in the evening. These stories were, as a rule, in English or German; he probably thought it was less frivolous to read these books in a foreign language. 'Silly nonsense,' he would say shrugging his shoulders; all the same he read them to the last line. Later, when Simenon's novels began to appear, he became an assiduous reader. 'Simenon is not bad at all,' he said. 'He describes French provincial life very well. That provincial atmosphere is very well done.'

But in the days of Via Pastrengo Simenon's books did not yet exist, and the books which my father brought back from his travels were glossy little volumes with pictures of ladies with their throats cut on the cover. When my mother found them in his overcoat pockets, she used to say, 'Look what silly nonsense our Beppino reads!'

Terni had created between Paola and Mario a kind of connivance which persisted even when he was not there. Their connivance was devoted, as far as I could make out, to the cult of melancholy. Paola and Mario went for melancholy walks in the twilight, either together or separately, in pensive solitude; or they read sad poems together, whispering in a doleful murmur.

Terni, however, if I remember rightly, was not at all a melancholy person. He was not particularly drawn to silent deserted places, and never went for brooding solitary walks. He lived in a perfectly normal way in his house with his wife Mary, the nanny Assunta, and his children Cucco and Lullina. He and his wife both spoilt them and would go into ecstasies over them. Terni had brought this taste for melancholy, and melancholy attitudes, into our house as he had introduced *La Nouvelle Revue Française* and Casorati's reproductions. Paola and Mario had responded but not Gino, whom Terni did not like and who did not like Terni at all; or Alberto, who could not care less about poetry or painting, and had never written another line since 'the old spin so flat and thin'. He only ever thought about playing football. Neither was I very interested in Terni, and only saw him as the father of Cucco, the boy with whom I sometimes played.

Lost in their melancholy, Paola and Mario were deeply resentful of their father's despotism, and the very simple austere habits in our house. They looked as if they felt exiled there, and were dreaming of a totally different home and a quite different way of life. Their resentment came out in long faces and moons, lifeless-looking eyes and impenetrable expressions, monosyllabic answers, bad-tempered door-slamming which shook the house, and a blank refusal to go mountaineering. Yet as soon as my father left the room they calmed down again, because their resentment did not include my mother, but was only directed at my father. They would listen to my mother's stories, and recite aloud with her the poem about the flood: 'Gazing in terror day by day they stood.'

Mario would have liked to read law but my father made him do economics and business studies. For some reason he did not think law was a very serious faculty, or that it offered secure prospects for the future. For years Mario bore an unspoken grudge against his father for this. As for Paola, she was generally discontented with the life she was leading, and would have liked to have more clothes. She did not like the clothes she had because they seemed too masculine and heavily cut. This was because my father insisted on us all having our clothes made by Maccheroni, the men's tailor, who was not expensive, or at least my father had convinced himself he was not. My mother had a little dressmaker called Alice, to whom she went occasionally, but she said she was not very good.

'I do wish I could have a pure silk dress,' my sister once said to my mother when they were chatting in the sitting-room. 'So do I,' said my mother. They were leafing through a fashion magazine. 'I should like,' said my mother, 'a nice pure silk "princesse".' 'So would I,' said my sister. But they could not buy pure silk because there was never enough money, and in any case Alice would have ruined it; she was no good at cutting out.

Paola would have liked to cut her hair, and to have high heels in place of those heavy masculine shoes made by 'Signor Castagneri'. She wanted to go to dances at friends' houses and to play tennis. She was not allowed to do any of these things. Instead she was more or less forced to go to the mountains every Saturday and Sunday with Gino and my father. Paola found Gino boring, Rasetti boring, and Gino's friends generally all very boring, and the mountains unbearable. However, she could ski very well. She had no style, they said, but she had a lot of stamina and great courage, and she flung herself down the slopes like a lioness. Judging by the fury and zest with which she flung herself down the slopes, I presume that she found skiing fun and thoroughly enjoyed herself. But she deeply despised mountaineering. She said she hated the hobnailed boots and the thick woollen socks, and the tiny freckles which the sun brought out on her delicate little nose. To get rid of her freckles after she had been mountaineering she used to cover her face with white powder. She would have liked to look frail and unhealthy, with a complexion as pale as the moon, like the women in Casorati's pictures, and she was annoyed when people told her she was 'as fresh as a rose'. When my father saw her white face, he never suspected that she was using powder, but said she was anaemic and he made her take iron. My father would wake up in the night and say to my mother, 'Paola and Mario have got such a moon. Those two have some pact together. I think that silly man Terni has set them against me.'

I never knew, and I still do not know, what Terni, Paola and Mario used to whisper about on that sofa in the sitting-room. Sometimes they really did talk about Proust. And then my mother would join in the conversation. *'La petite phrase,'* she would say. 'It is so good when he talks about the *petite phrase.* Silvio would have liked it so

55

much too!' Terni took out his monocle and rubbed it in his handkerchief like Swann, and went 'sst, sst'.

'What great writing! What marvellous writing!' Terni always said, and Paola and my mother would mimic him all day long. 'Twaddle,' my father said when he picked up some words as he went by, 'I am sick of all your twaddle!' He went straight on into his study, and when he got there he shouted 'Terni! You still have not finished your work on tissue pathology. You waste too much time on silly nonsense. You are lazy, you don't do enough work. You are a great lazybones!'

Paola was in love with one of her university friends.[9] He was small and delicate, and had an attractive voice. They went for walks together on the riverside or in the Valentino Gardens, and talked about Proust, as the young man was an ardent Proustian; in fact he was the first person in Italy to write about Proust. He wrote stories and critical essays. I think Paola was in love with him because he was the exact opposite of my father; so small and kind, such a sweet attractive voice. And he knew nothing about tissue pathology and had never set foot on a ski slope. My father came to know about these walks and was furious in the first place because his daughters ought not to go for walks with men; and then because to him a man of letters, a critic, a writer, was something contemptible, frivolous and even doubtful — it was a world that repelled him. All the same Paola continued to take these walks, in spite of her father's prohibition. Sometimes they met the Lopezes or other friends of my parents who told my father, since they knew he had forbidden them. But Terni never gave her away to her father if he met her, because Paola had confided in him in their whisperings on the sofa.

'Don't let her go out!' shouted my father to my mother. 'Do not let her go out! Forbid her to go out!' My mother was not happy about these walks either, and distrusted the young man too. This was because my father had infected her with a confused and inarticulate repugnance for the world of letters, a world unknown in our house, as only biologists, scientists and engineers came into it. Besides, my mother was very close to Paola and before this affair with the young man they used to go into town together and look at pure silk dresses in the shop windows, which neither of them could buy. But now Paola was rarely free to go out with my mother, and when she was

56

free, and they went out, chatting arm in arm, they ended up talking about her young man and returned home in a temper, because my mother was not as nice or as welcoming to the young man, whom she hardly knew anyway, as Paola demanded. But my mother was quite incapable of forbidding anyone anything. 'You have no authority,' my father would shout and wake her up in the night. But she had shown that he had no authority either, for Paola went on going for walks with her young man for years, and only stopped when the affair died out by itself, like a candle going out, and not because of anything to do with my father's shouting and vetoes.

My father lost his temper not only over Paola and her young man but also because of my brother Alberto's work. Instead of doing his homework he always went off to play football. The only sport my father would recognize was mountaineering. He thought other forms of sport were social and frivolous, like tennis, or stupid and boring, like swimming (he hated the sea — beaches and sand). Football, he reckoned, was a game for street urchins and he would not count it as a sport at all.

Gino worked hard at school and so did Mario. Paola did no work at all but that did not worry my father. She was a girl, and my father thought that it did not matter if girls did not try at school, as they would get married afterwards. With me he did not even know that I was not learning any arithmetic. Only my mother was in despair about it, as she had a duty to teach me. Alberto did no work at all, and my father having been ill-prepared for this by his other sons' behaviour got into a terrifying rage when he came home with a bad report or was sent home from school for misbehaving.

My father was concerned about all his sons' futures, and often woke up in the night to ask my mother, 'What is Gino going to do? What is Mario going to do?' But my father was not just concerned about Alberto, who was still at school: he was positively panic-stricken. 'That scoundrel Alberto! That rascal Alberto!' He never said 'That ass Alberto!' because Alberto was worse than an ass; he thought his behaviour monstrous and unheard of. Alberto spent his days either on the football field, from which he would return covered in mud, and sometimes with his knees or his head blood-stained and bandaged, or out with his friends, and he was always late for dinner. My father would sit down and start banging his glass, his fork and his bread on the table, and one could not tell whether he was annoyed with Mussolini or with Alberto who had not yet come in. 'A rascal! A scoundrel!' he would say while Natalina came in with the soup, and he would get more and more angry as lunch went on. At dessert Alberto would appear, cool, rosy, smiling. Alberto never had sulky moods and was always cheerful. 'You scoundrel! Where have you been?' my father bellowed. 'At school,' answered Alberto coolly. 'Then I went home with one of my friends.' 'One of your friends! You are nothing but a rascal! It is after the *bell*!' One o'clock was for my father the bell, and to come in after the bell he thought was outrageous.

My mother complained about Alberto too. 'He is always dirty,' she said. 'He wanders around like a tramp. He is for ever asking me for money, and he never does any work.'

'I am going round to see my friend Pajetta[10] for a bit. I am going to see my friend Pestelli for a bit. Could you let me have two lire please, Mama?' That is what Alberto said at home, and he did not say much else. This was not because he was not communicative (in fact, he was the most communicative, expansive and cheerful of us), but merely because he was never at home. 'Always Pajetta! Pajetta! Pajetta!' my mother would say, uttering the name fast and angrily, possibly to indicate the speed at which Alberto ran off. Even in those days two lire was a small sum, but Alberto used to ask for two lire several times a day. My mother would sigh and unlock her desk drawer. But Alberto never had enough money. He took to selling our books so the book-cases were gradually emptied. Every now and again my father would look for a book and not be able to find it, and so that he would not get angry my mother would say that she had lent it to Frances, although we knew quite well that it had ended up on a second-hand bookstall. Alberto even sometimes took some of our silver to the pawn-broker; and when she could not find a coffee-pot my mother began to cry. 'You see what Alberto has done!' she would say to Paola. 'You see what he has done to me. But I cannot tell Papa, or he will shout at him.' She was so terrified of my father's fits of anger that she used to find the pawn-tickets in Alberto's drawer, and send Rina to redeem her coffee-pot in secret without telling my father.

Alberto was no longer friends with Frinco, who had disappeared into the mists of time with his thrillers, he was not even friends with Frances's children. He now had his schoolfriends, Pajetta and

58

Pestelli, but they did work. My mother always said that Alberto chose friends who were better than himself. 'Pestelli,' she explained to my father, 'is an excellent character. He comes from a very good family. His father is the Pestelli who writes for *La Stampa*[11] and his mother is Carola Prosperi,' she said with satisfaction and in order to put Alberto in a good light in my father's eyes. Carola Prosperi was a writer whom my mother liked, and she did not think she would be part of the untrustworthy world of literary people because she wrote books for children; her novels, the ones for grown-ups, were, so my mother always said, 'very well written'. My father, who had never read any of Carola Prosperi's books, shrugged his shoulders.

As for Pajetta, he was still a small boy in shorts at school when he was arrested for circulating anti-Fascist pamphlets in the class-room, and Alberto, who was one of his closest friends, was summoned to the police station for interrogation. Pajetta was locked up and put into a reformatory for minors, and my mother, feeling rather flattered, said to my father: 'You see what I told you, Beppino. You see that Alberto always chooses his friends well. They are always finer characters and more serious than he is.'

My father shrugged his shoulders. He was, all the same, rather flattered that Alberto should have been interrogated by the police, and for days refrained from calling him a scoundrel.

'You tramp!' said my mother when Alberto came back from football, dirty, with his fair hair caked in mud and his clothes torn. 'You tramp!'

'He smokes and knocks the ash on the floor,' she complained to her friends. 'He lies on the ' ed with his boots on and dirties the bedspread. He is always asking for money, and he never has enough. He was so sweet when he was little, so soft and gentle. He was a little lamb. I used to dress him up in lace. He had such pretty curls. And now look what he has turned into.'

Alberto's and Mario's friends seldom appeared at our house. But Gino always brought his friends for the evening. My father invited them to stay to supper. He was always ready to ask people to lunch or to supper, and sometimes there might not be much to eat. On the other hand, he was always afraid that we might 'scrounge meals' in other people's houses. 'You scrounged lunch off Frances? I am not at all pleased.' If one of us was asked out to a meal and the next day said that the person was boring or unpleasant, he would protest immediately: 'Uncongenial! But you scrounged lunch off them!'

Our supper usually consisted of Liebig's soup, which my mother was very fond of and which Natalina always made too thin, and an omelette. So Gino's friends shared these suppers with us, which were always the same, and sat around the table listening to my mother's anecdotes and songs. Among these friends was one called Adriano Olivetti.[12] I remember the first time he came to the house in uniform, since he was doing his military service. So was Gino just then, and he and Adriano were in the same dormitory. Adriano at that time had a reddish beard which was unkempt and curly, and he had long, fair reddish hair which curled down his neck. He was pale and fat. His uniform fitted badly on his fat round shoulders and I have never seen anyone in grey-green uniform with a pistol at his belt who looked more goofy and less soldierly than he did. He looked very depressed, probably because he did not at all like being a soldier. He was diffident and taciturn, and when he did speak, he spoke slowly in a very quiet voice, and said a lot of confused obscure things while he gazed into space with his little blue eyes, at once cold and dreamy. At that time Adriano seemed to be the incarnation of what my father used to call 'a layabout'. Yet my father never said that he was a layabout, a sausage or a '*negro*'. He never used any of these words about Adriano. I wonder why? I think that probably my father had more insight into character than we suspected, and that he could see through the outward garb of this embarrassed youth to an impression of the man that Adriano was to develop into later. Yet possibly the only reason for not calling him a layabout was that he was a mountaineer; and also because Gino had told him that Adriano was an anti-Fascist, and that he was the son of a Socialist who was like him a friend of Turati.

The Olivettis had a typewriter factory at Ivrea. We had never known any industrialists till then. The only industrialist who was ever mentioned in our house was a brother of Lopez, named Mauro. He lived in Argentina and was very rich. My father had it in mind to send Gino to work in Mauro's business. The Olivettis were the first industrialists that we saw at close quarters and it made a big impression on me to think that the advertisements I saw in the street with a typewriter running on a railway track were closely connected with that Adriano in a grey-green uniform who often ate our tasteless soup with us in the evening.

After his military service was over Adriano continued to come to supper with us, and was even more depressed, shy and taciturn. He was in love with my sister Paola, who at that time paid no attention to him. Adriano owned a motor-car, and was the only one among our acquaintances to do so. Even Terni, who was so rich, did not possess a car. When my father had to go out somewhere, Adriano would immediately offer to take him in his car, and that made my father very angry. He could not stand motor-cars, nor, he always said, acts of kindness.

Adriano had many brothers and sisters, all with freckles and red hair, and perhaps my father may have liked them partly because he too had freckles and red hair. We all knew that they were very rich, but all the same they lived very simply. They dressed quietly, and went to the mountains with old skis just as we did. They had several cars and were constantly offering to take us to one place or another, and when they were driving in town and saw an elderly person walking along who looked tired, they would stop and ask him to get in. My mother was always saying how good and kind they were.

In due course we came to know their father as well. He was a little stout man with a big white beard; in the middle of the beard he had a handsome, delicate, noble face, with shining blue eyes. He used to fiddle with his beard as he spoke, and with his waistcoat buttons. He had a small falsetto voice, rather sharp and childlike. Perhaps because of his white beard my father always referred to him as 'old Olivetti', though actually they were both about the same age. Both being socialist, and friends of Turati, they respected and admired one another. However, when they met both always wanted to talk at the same time and they shouted at each other, one in falsetto, the other one bellowing. Old Olivetti's conversation was a mixture of the Bible, psychoanalysis and the preachings of the prophets. These were topics absolutely outside my father's world, about which he had formed no special opinion. He considered that Olivetti was very intelligent but had very confused ideas.

The Olivetti family lived at Ivrea in a house called The Convent, because it had once been a convent. They had woods and vineyards, cows and cattle sheds. Thanks to these cows they had cream cakes every day. We had a passion for cream which went back to the days

61

in the mountains when my father had forbidden us to stop and eat at the chalets. He forbade it among other things for fear of brucellosis. At the Olivettis, with their own cows, there was no danger of brucellosis, so when we were there we could let ourselves go on the cream. All the same my father used to say, 'You must not always get yourselves invited to the Olivettis. You must not scrounge!' The result was we were so obsessed about scrounging that on one occasion Gino and Paola having been invited to spend the day at Ivrea refused to stay to supper however much the Olivettis insisted, or even to be brought back in their car. They slipped away with empty stomachs and waited for the train in the dark. Another time I happened to have to travel with the Olivettis by car, and we stopped at a restaurant for dinner, and while they all ordered *tagliatelle* and steaks, I asked for a boiled egg only, and later told my sister that I had asked for an egg 'because I did not want Signor Olivetti to spend too much'. This came to the old gentleman's ears, and he was very amused and often used to laugh about it. He laughed at it in delight at being very rich and knowing it and discovering that there was still someone who did not know.

When Gino finished at the Polytechnic two possibilities were open to him. He could either go and work with Mauro who had a business in Argentina, and whom we called 'Uncle Mauro', familiarly copying the Lopez boys; and in fact my father had been corresponding for months with Uncle Mauro about Gino's future. Or he could go and work at Signor Olivetti's factory at Ivrea. Gino chose the latter.

So Gino left home and went to live at Ivrea, and after a few months he announced to my father that he had met a girl there and was engaged to her. My father was violently angry. He was always violently angry every time one of us announced that we were about to marry, never mind who the chosen person was. He always found some excuse. He would say that the person of our choice had poor health, had no money, or had too much money. On each occasion he forbade the marriage, which did not achieve anything because we all married just the same.

So Gino was then sent to Germany to learn the language and to forget. My mother advised him to go and call on Signora Grassi at Freiburg. This lady was my mother's childhood friend who used to say, 'All wool, Lydia!' and 'the violets, Lydia!' In Florence she had

62

met a bookseller from Freiburg and had married him. He used to read Heine to her and taught her to love violets. And he taught her to love 'pure wool' material by taking her back to Germany after the 1914–18 war at a time when pure wool was not to be found in Germany. When he got back to Freiburg after the war, he exclaimed, 'I do not recognize Germany any more!' This remark remained famous in our family, and my mother used to quote it whenever she failed to recognize some one or something.

That summer in the mountains my father wrote a lot of letters to Gino in Germany and to the Ternis, the Lopezes and to Signor Olivetti, all to do with the marriage, and to each of them my father wrote that they ought to dissuade Gino from marrying, at the age of twenty-five and with no settled career.

'I wonder if he has seen Signora Grassi,' my mother would say now and again that summer, and my father would answer angrily: 'Signora Grassi! A lot I care whether he has seen Signora Grassi. You would think your Signora Grassi was the only person in Germany. I refuse to let Gino get married.'

However, Gino got married on his return from Germany, as he had said he would, and my father and mother went to the wedding. Yet my father still woke up in the night and said, 'If only I had sent him to Mauro in Argentina instead of to Ivrea! Who knows, perhaps he would not have got married in Argentina.'

We had now moved house, and my mother who had always complained about the house in Via Pastrengo now complained about the new house in Via Pallamaglio. 'What an ugly name!' she was always saying. 'What an ugly street! I cannot bear these streets, Via Campana, Via Saluzzo. At least we had a garden in Via Pastrengo.'

The new flat was on the top floor and looked on to a piazza in which there was a large ugly church, a varnish factory and public baths. In my mother's eyes nothing was more squalid than the sight from our windows of men going to these baths with towels under their arms. My father had bought this flat outright because he said it did not cost much, and though it was not wonderful it had advantages; it was near the station, and was large, with plenty of rooms.

'What does it matter if we are near the station?' my mother said. 'We never go away.'

There must have been some improvement in our economic situation, for there was less talk about money. The Property shares were always going down, if one listened to my father, and must by now, I thought, have been engulfed in the bowels of the earth. Nevertheless my mother and sister had more clothes. And now we had the telephone too, like the Lopezes. Food prices and the high cost of living were no longer mentioned. Gino was living with his wife at Ivrea. Mario had a job in Genoa and only came home on Saturdays.

After a great deal of debate and uncertainty Alberto had been sent to boarding-school. My father hoped that he would be unhappy there and with this severe punishment would repent and have a change of heart. But my mother said to Alberto: 'I'm sure you'll like it! I'm sure you will enjoy yourself. When I was at boarding-school it was lovely. I had such fun.'

Alberto went off to school as cheerfully as ever. When he came home for the holidays he told us that when they were at table eating omelettes a bell rang. The headmaster entered the room and said, 'I would remind you that one does not cut an omelette with a knife!' Then the bell rang again and the headmaster disappeared. My father no longer went skiing. He said he was too old. My mother had always said: 'The mountains! What a hole!' She could not ski, of course, but stayed indoors. But now she was sorry that her husband did not go skiing any more.

Anna Kulischov had died. My mother had not seen her for many years but she had been happy to know that she was still alive. She went to Milan for the funeral with her friend Paola Carrara who had also spent a lot of time at the Kulischovs when she was a little girl. She brought home a book with a black border which contained writings in memory of Madame Kulischov, and portraits of her.

So my mother saw Milan again after all these years. But she no longer knew anyone there. Her family were all dead. The city had changed and become ugly. 'I do not recognize Germany any more!' she said.

The Ternis were to leave Turin and live in Florence. Mary went first with the children. Terni stayed on for a few months. 'What a pity that you are leaving Turin,' said my mother to Terni. 'What a pity Mary has gone. I shall not see the children any more. Do you remember the garden in Via Pastrengo when you played ball with

Cucco? And Gino's friends came and we played grandmother's footsteps. It was lovely!'

'I don't like this house,' my mother said. 'I don't like Via Pallamaglio. I liked having a garden.'

Her depression, however, soon passed. She got up in the morning singing and organized the shopping. Then she took the No. 7 tram, and went right to the end of the line and back without getting off. 'It's lovely sitting on a tram! Much nicer than going in a car.'

'You must come too,' she would say to me in the morning. 'Let us go to Pozzo Strada.' At Pozzo Strada, the end of the No. 7 line, there was a wide space with an ice-cream kiosk, the last houses at the edge of the city, and in the distance fields of corn and poppies.

In the afternoon she stretched out on a sofa and read the paper. She would say to me, 'If you are good, I will take you to the cinema. Let us see if there is a film suitable for you.' It was she, however, who really wanted to go to the cinema, and in fact she often went there alone or with her friends if I had some homework to do.

She came running back because my father returned from the laboratory at half-past seven and expected to find her at home on his return. If she was not there, he stood on the balcony waiting for her. My mother arrived out of breath, with her hat in her hand. 'Where the devil have you been?' my father shouted. 'You have worried me, I bet you have been to the cinema again today. You spend your life at the cinema.'

'Have you written to Mary?' he would ask. Now that Mary had gone to live in Florence, letters from her arrived from time to time. My mother never remembered to answer them. She was very fond of Mary, but she never felt like writing letters. She did not even write to her sons.

'Have you written to Gino?' my father would shout. 'Write to Gino. You watch out if you don't write to Gino!'

I got ill, and was ill all winter. I had an ear infection then mastoiditis. My father looked after me himself the first few days. In his study he kept a small cupboard which he called 'the chemist's' and in it there were a few medicines and instruments which he used to treat his children, his friends and their children. There was tincture of iodine for cuts and abrasions; for sore throats blue meths; for whitlows the '*bir*'. The *bir* was a rubber band which had to be tied tightly round the ailing finger until it turned blue.

65

The *bir*, however, could never be found in 'the chemist's' when it was needed, and my father went round the house shouting: 'Where is the *bir*? Where have you put the *bir*? You are so untidy! I have never seen anyone as untidy as you lot!'

The *bir* was generally found in a drawer in his desk.

In spite of all this he got angry if anyone asked his advice about their health, and he would say huffily: 'I'm not a doctor, you know.' He was willing to treat people but only on condition that they did not ask to be treated.

He said one day at table, 'That silly man Terni has influenza. He has put himself to bed. Pooh! There cannot be anything wrong with him. I must go and see him!'

'That man Terni really does exaggerate!' he said in the evening. 'There is nothing the matter with him. He is lying in bed with a woollen vest on. I never wear woollen vests!'

After some days he said, 'I am rather worried about Terni. His temperature will not go down. I'm afraid he may have a pleural discharge. I want Stroppeni to see him.'

'He has had a pleural discharge,' he shouted when he came home that evening and looked for my mother in all the rooms. 'Do you know, Lydia, Terni has had a pleural discharge.'

He brought Stroppeni and all the doctors he knew to Terni's bedside.

'Don't smoke,' he shouted to Terni when he was better and was sitting in the sun on his veranda. 'You realize you should not smoke, you smoke too much, you have always smoked too much. You have ruined your health by smoking too much.'

My father himself smoked like a chimney, but he did not want other people to do so.

When his friends or his children were ill he became kind and gentle. But as soon as they were well again he went back to bullying them.

I was seriously ill: my father very quickly gave up treating me and called in doctors whom he could trust. Eventually I was taken to hospital. So that I would not be upset my mother gave me to understand that the hospital was the doctor's house, and that the other patients in the wards were his children, cousins, nephews and nieces. I obediently believed her; but at the same time I really knew

66

that it was a hospital; on that occasion and again later, truth and lies got mixed up.

This was because Frances used to compare Lucio's legs with mine, and be worried how thin and pale his legs were in his white socks with black velvet garters.

ONE evening I heard my mother talking to someone in the hall. I heard her open the linen-cupboard. Shadows moved across the glass panels of the door.

In the night I heard someone coughing in the room next to me — the room used by Mario when he came home on Saturdays. But this could not be Mario because it was not Saturday, and it sounded like the cough of an old, heavily-built man.

My mother came to me in the morning and told me that someone called Signor Paolo Ferrari had slept there, and that he was tired and old and coughed, and one must not ask him too many questions.

Signor Paolo Ferrari was in the dining-room drinking tea. On seeing him I recognized Turati who had once come to us at Via Pastrengo. But as I had been told that he was called Paolo Ferrari, I believed, obediently, that he was at the same time both Turati and Ferrari, and once more truth and lies got mixed up.

Ferrari was old, as huge as a bear, with a grey goatee beard. He had a very big collar size and a tie like a piece of string. He had small white hands, and he was leafing through a volume of Carducci's poems, bound in red.

Then he did a strange thing. He took Madame Kulischov's memorial volume and wrote in it a long dedication to my mother, and signed it 'Anna and Filippo'. This added greatly to my confusion. I could not understand how he could be Anna and also Filippo if in fact he was, as they said, Paolo Ferrari.

My father and mother appeared very pleased he was there. My father did not lose his temper, and everyone spoke in subdued tones. Every time the bell rang Paolo Ferrari ran down the passage and took refuge in a room at the end. It was usually Lucio or the milkman. We had no other visitors.

He ran down the passage, trying to go on tiptoe, like a great shadow of a bear on the walls.

Paola said to me, 'His name is not Ferrari, it is Turati. He has to escape from Italy. He is in hiding. You must not tell anybody not even Lucio.'

I swore not to say anything to anyone, not even to Lucio. But I very much wanted to tell Lucio when he came to play with me. Lucio, however, was not at all inquisitive. He always said I was 'being inquisitive' when I tried to question him about things at his house. The Lopezes were all secretive and did not like to talk about family matters, so we never knew whether they were rich or poor, or how old Frances was, or even what they had for dinner.

Lucio said to me casually, 'There is a man here in your house with a beard who rushes out of the sitting-room as soon as I arrive.'

'Yes,' said I, 'Paolo Ferrari.'

I wanted him to ask me more questions, but Lucio did not ask anything else. He was hammering a nail in the wall to put up a picture which he had painted and was giving me. It was a picture of a train. Lucio had been mad on trains since he was little, and used to run round the room puffing and panting like a locomotive. At home he had a big electric train which his uncle Mauro had sent him from Argentina.

I said to Lucio, 'Don't hammer like that. He is old and ill and hiding. We must not disturb him.'

'Who?'

'Paolo Ferrari!'

'You see the tender,' said Lucio, 'you see I have painted the tender too.'

Lucio always talked about the tender. I got rather bored when I was with him nowadays. We were the same age but he always seemed much smaller than me. Still I did not want him to go away. When Maria Buoninsegni came to fetch him I would make a scene and get her to let him stay a little longer.

Lucio and I were sent down to the piazza with Natalina to wait for Maria Buoninsegni. My mother said it would give us some fresh air. But I knew it was so that Maria Buoninsegni should not meet Paolo Ferrari in the passage.

In the middle of the piazza there was a rectangle of grass and some benches. Natalina sat on one of them swinging her short legs with long feet. Lucio played trains round the piazza, puffing and panting as he went.

When Maria Buoninsegni arrived, with her fox, Natalina was all politeness and smiles. She felt the greatest admiration for Maria. But Maria hardly looked at her, only talked to Lucio in her precise, classy

69

Tuscan accent. She made him put on his pullover, since he was very hot.

Paolo Ferrari stayed in our house for eight or ten days, I think. They were strangely quiet days. I heard a good deal of talk about a motor-boat. One evening we had supper early and I understood that he was to leave us. During those days he had been cheerful and calm, but that night at supper he appeared nervous and scratched his beard.

Then two or three men in raincoats came. Adriano was the only one I knew. He was starting to lose his hair and had an almost bald square head, surrounded by fair, curly locks. That evening his face and scanty hair looked wind-swept. His eyes seemed alarmed, but resolute and cheerful. Two or three times in my life I saw that look in his eyes. It was the look he had when he was helping someone to escape, when there was danger and someone to be taken to safety.

Paolo Ferrari said while I was helping him on with his overcoat in the hall: 'Don't tell a soul that I have been here.'

He went out with Adriano and the other men in raincoats, and I never saw him again. He died in Paris a few years later.

The next day Natalina asked my mother, 'He will have got to Corsica by now, in that boat, won't he?'

My father heard these words and was furious with my mother: 'You have gone and confided in that lunatic Natalina. She's a lunatic, she will land us all in prison!'

'No, no, Beppino. Natalina knows very well that she must keep quiet.'

Presently a postcard came from Corsica with greetings from Paolo Ferrari.

In the months that followed I heard Rosselli[13] and Parri,[14] who had helped Turati to escape, had been arrested. Adriano was still at liberty but in danger, they said, and might come to our house to hide there.

Adriano hid in our house for several months and slept in Mario's room, where Paolo Ferrari had slept. Ferrari was safe in Paris. But now they were tired of calling him Ferrari and used his real name. My mother said, 'He was so nice! I did so like having him here!'

Adriano was not arrested, and went abroad. He and my sister used to write to each other, as they were now engaged. Old Olivetti came to see my parents to ask on behalf of his son for my sister's hand in marriage. He came from Ivrea on a motor-cycle, wearing a peaked cap. He had plastered his chest with newspapers to keep out the wind, as he always did when riding a motor-cycle. He asked for my sister's hand in no time but then stayed a bit longer in an armchair in our sitting-room, fiddling with his beard and talking about himself. He told us how he had built up his factory with very little money, how he had brought up his children, and how he read the Bible every night before he went to sleep.

My father now lost his temper with my mother because he did not want this marriage. He said that Adriano was too rich and also too preoccupied with psychoanalysis, as indeed were all the Olivettis. My father liked them all well enough, but considered them rather eccentric. The Olivettis said we were too materialistic, especially my father and Gino.

After some time we realized that we would not be arrested; nor would Adriano, who came back from abroad and married my sister Paola. As soon as my sister was married she cut her hair short. My father said nothing because now he could not say anything any more, he could not forbid her or tell her to do things. All the same he began to scold her again after a while, in fact now he scolded Adriano too. He found that they spent too much, and motored too frequently between Ivrea and Turin.

When their first child, a boy, arrived he criticized the way he was brought up. He thought he should get more sun, or he would get rickets. 'They will give him rickets,' he shouted to my mother. 'They don't put him in the sun. They should put him in the sun!'

Then he was afraid that if the baby was ill they would take him to quack doctors. Adriano had not much faith in real doctors, and on one occasion when he had had sciatica he had gone to a Bulgarian for aerial massage. He had asked my father his opinion of aerial massage, and whether he knew the Bulgarian. My father knew nothing of the Bulgarian, and the idea of aerial massage made him lose his temper. 'He must be a charlatan! A quack!' he cried. When the baby had a slight temperature he became worried. 'They will take him to some quack, won't they?' he said.

He liked this baby, Roberto, very much and thought he was beautiful; he laughed when he looked at him because he thought he looked just like old Olivetti. 'He is exactly like the old man.' 'You would think it was old Olivetti!' my mother said too.

71

The moment Paola arrived from Ivrea he would say, 'Tell me about Roberto.' 'He is a beautiful baby, Roberto,' he was always saying. Then Paola had another baby, a girl, but he did not like her. When the baby was shown to him he hardly looked at her. 'Roberto is more beautiful,' he said. Paola was offended and put on a face. When she had gone he said to my mother, 'You see what an ass she is, Paola!'

In the early days of Paola's marriage, my mother cried a lot because she no longer had her at home. There was a great bond between them and they always had a great deal to say to each other. My mother never said anything to me; in her eyes I was too small and she said that I 'did not give her a chance'.

I went to secondary school now, and she was not teaching me arithmetic any more. I still could not understand the subject but she was unable to help because she could not remember secondary school arithmetic.

'She never unwinds. She does not speak,' she said of me. The only thing that she could do with me was to take me to the cinema. But I did not always accept her requests to go with her.

'I do not know what my mistress will do,' 'now I know what my mistress wishes to do,' she would say over the telephone to her friends. She always called me her 'mistress', because, in fact, it was I who was the one to decide how we should spend the afternoon, whether or not I should agree to go to the cinema.

'I am fed up,' my mother said. 'I have nothing to do any more, there is nothing to do in this house now. They have all gone away, and I am fed up.'

'You are fed up,' said my father, 'because you have no inner life.'

'My little Mario!' she exclaimed. 'Thank goodness it is Saturday today, and my little Mario will be coming.'

Mario indeed came nearly every Saturday. He would open his suitcase on the bed in the room where Ferrari had slept, and with meticulous care take out silk pyjamas, cakes of soap and morocco slippers. He always had beautiful smart new things, and good clothes in English materials. 'All wool, Lydia,' my mother would say as she fingered the material of these clothes.

'Eh! you have your little things too,' she would say, mimicking my aunt Drusilla.

Mario would still say '*Il baco del calo del malo*' while he sat for a

72

moment with my mother and me in the sitting-room, rubbing his jaw. Then suddenly he would go to the telephone and make mysterious appointments in a low voice. 'Good-bye, Mama!' he would cry from the hall and we would not see him again until suppertime.

Mario seldom brought his friends to the house, and when they came he did not bring them into the sitting-room but shut himself up with them in his own room. They were all men with a serious and businesslike air, and Mario himself always seemed serious and businesslike. He seemed to think of nothing but his business career, and nothing else mattered. He was no longer friends with Terni, and he no longer read Proust or Verlaine. He only read books on economics and finance. He spent his holidays abroad, travelling on cruises, and no longer came with us in the summer. He went off on his own account, and at times we did not even know where he was.

'Where can Mario be?' asked my father when he had not written for some time. 'We don't know anything about him, we don't know what sort of life he leads. What an ass!'

We knew, however, from Paola that Mario often went to Switzerland; not, however, to ski. He had never again put skis on his feet from the day he left home. He had a girl friend in Switzerland, as thin as thin — she weighed less than six stone — because he only liked women who were very thin and very elegant. According to Paola, this lady had a hot bath two or three times a day; and Mario too did nothing but have baths, shave and scent himself with lavender water. He was always afraid of being dirty or smelling bad. Everything disgusted him, rather as it had my grandmother. When Natalina brought him coffee he would examine the cup all over to make sure it had been properly washed.

'I should like him to marry some nice little girl,' my mother said every now and then. This made my father furious at once. 'What! Get married! What next? I will not hear of Mario getting married!'

MY GRANDMOTHER died, and we all went to Florence for the funeral. She was buried there in the family tomb beside grandfather Parente, 'poor little Regina' and all the other Margheritas and Reginas.

Henceforth my father always referred to her in a particularly affectionate and commiserating tone as 'my poor mother'. When she was alive he had always tended to call her stupid, as he did with all of us. But now that she was dead her faults seemed to him innocent and childlike, deserving of pity and sympathy.

She bequeathed her furniture to us. My father said it was of 'great value', but my mother did not like it. However, Gino's wife, Piera, also said it was good. My mother was rather shaken. She had confidence in Piera who, she said, knew a great deal about furniture. Still she found it too big and heavy. There were some armchairs which grandfather Parente had brought over from India, made of carved black wood, with elephants' heads on the arm-rests. There were small chairs in black and gold — Chinese I believe — and a quantity of knick-knacks and china; and silver and plates with a crest which had once belonged to our Dormitzer cousins, who had been made barons after lending money to the Austrian Emperor Franz-Joseph.

My mother was afraid that when Alberto came home for the holidays he would take something to the pawnbroker. So she had a small cabinet made with a locking glass front, and there she placed all the smaller pieces of porcelain. She maintained, however, that my grandmother's furniture did not suit our house; it got in the way and did not look good. 'It is not the sort of furniture,' she said every day, 'that goes with Via Pallamaglio.'

So my father decided that we should move again, and we went to live in the Corso Re Umberto. We had a ground-floor apartment in a low old house overlooking the Corso. My mother was very pleased to be on the ground floor once more because she felt nearer to the street; she could go in and out without going up and down stairs, and without a hat, as she always dreamed of going out without a hat, although her husband had forbidden her to do so.

'But in Palermo,' she said, 'I always went out without a hat.'

'Palermo! Palermo! Palermo! That was fifteen years ago. Look at Frances, she never goes out without a hat.'

Alberto left boarding-school and came to Turin for his school-leaving certificate examination. He did very well and had excellent marks. We were all astonished.

'You see what I told you, Beppino!' said my mother. 'You see he can work when he wants to.'

'And now,' said my father, 'what shall we do with him now?'

'But what are you going to do with Alberto?' my mother said, poking fun at Aunt Drusilla, who always said that to a son of hers who did nothing at school, and my mother used to say to her, 'What are you going to do with Andrea?' (Aunt Drusilla was the one who used to say 'But you have your little wardrobe.') Sometimes she joined us in the summer; she rented a house near ours, and she showed my mother her son's clothes and said, 'Andrea has a little wardrobe too.' Immediately she arrived in the mountains she went to the farm that sold milk and said, 'I am actually prepared to pay a little more, but I want you to deliver the milk to me before the others.' The upshot was that they brought the milk to her at the same time as to us, but they made her pay more for it.

'But what are you going to do with Alberto?' my mother kept asking all the summer. Aunt Drusilla was not with us that year since she had some time ago given up joining us in the mountains, but my mother still had her voice echoing in her ears. Alberto when he was asked said he was going to read medicine.

He said this with a casual resigned air, shrugging his shoulders. Alberto was now a tall, thin, fair-haired youth with a long nose — a success with the girls. When my mother rummaged in his drawers for pawn-tickets she found a heap of letters from girls, and photographs.

He did not see Pestelli any more now that he was married, nor Pajetta, who after his time at the approved school had been arrested once more, tried by the Political Offences court and sent to prison at Civitavecchia. Alberto now had a friend called Vittorio.[15]

'That Vittorio,' said my mother, 'is an excellent boy, he works very hard. He comes from a very good family. Alberto is a slacker but he always chooses his friends well.' Alberto had not ceased to be, in my mother's parlance, a 'tramp' and a 'slacker' — though I don't quite know what she meant — even after he had passed his leaving certificate exam.

'Scoundrel! Rascal!' my father shouted when Alberto came home at night. He was so accustomed to shouting that he did so even when Alberto happened to come in early. 'But where the devil have you been this late?' 'I have just been seeing a friend of mine home,' Alberto would reply in a bright breezy voice.

Alberto ran after little milliners, but he chased respectable girls as well. He ran after all the girls, for he liked them all, and because he was so cheerful and kind he even courted the ones he did not like, through sheer kindness of heart. He enrolled for medicine, and when my father found Alberto in his anatomy class he didn't much like it. There was one occasion when the room was dark and my father was showing some slides; he saw the glow of a cigarette in the darkness. 'Who is smoking?' he shouted. 'What son of a dog has started smoking?' 'It's me, papa,' said the familiar voice, and everybody laughed.

When Alberto had to sit an examination my father was in a terrible mood from first thing in the morning. 'He will show me up badly. He has not done any work at all!' he said to my mother. 'Wait, Beppino, wait!' she said. 'We don't know yet.'

'He got an A,' my mother told him. 'An A?' he was furious. 'An A? They gave him that because he is my son. If he were not my son, they would have failed him.' And he was angrier than ever.

Later Alberto became a very good doctor. But my father was never convinced, and when my mother or one of us was not well, and wished to send for Alberto, my father would bellow with laughter, 'What! Alberto! What do you expect him to know?'

Alberto and his friend Vittorio used to stroll along the Corso Re Umberto. Vittorio had black hair, square shoulders and a long prominent chin. Alberto had fair hair, a long nose, and a short receding chin. They talked about girls, also about politics, because Vittorio was a political conspirator. Alberto was not at all interested in politics; he did not read the papers, expressed no opinions, and never took any part in the arguments which still erupted between my father and Mario. But he was attracted by conspirators. From the time when he and Pajetta were boys in shorts, Alberto had been attracted by conspiracies without, however, taking part in them. He

76

liked to be the friend and confidant of conspirators.

When my father met Alberto and Vittorio on the Corso he nodded to them curtly. It never entered his head that one of them could be a conspirator and the other his confidant. Besides, the people he was used to seeing with Alberto only filled him with suspicion and contempt. He did not think that there were any conspirators left in Italy. He believed that he himself was one of the very few anti-Fascists remaining in the country. The others were the people he used to meet in Paola Carrara's house, my mother's friend who had been, like her, a friend of Kulischov.

'This evening,' said my father to my mother, 'we are going to the Carraras. Salvatorelli[16] will be there.'

'Oh, lovely! I am really curious to hear what Salvatorelli says.'

After spending an evening with Salvatorelli, in Paola Carrara's little sitting-room which was full of dolls which she made for a charity in which she was interested, my father and mother felt reassured. Nothing new had been said really. But many of my parents' friends had become Fascists, or at least were not so openly and avowedly anti-Fascist as they would have liked. So they felt increasingly lonely as the year went by.

Salvatorelli, the Carraras, and old Olivetti, were in my father's opinion the few anti-Fascists left in the world. They, like himself, preserved memories of the days of Turati and of a way of life which seemed to have been swept off the face of the earth. Being with them was a breath of fresh air for my father. Then there were Vinciguerra,[17] Bauer[18] and Rossi,[19] who had been in prison for years, having plotted against Fascism in earlier days. My father thought of them with a mixture of veneration and despair, since he didn't believe they would ever be released. Then there were the Communists, but my father did not know any of them, except Pajetta, whom he remembered as a little boy in shorts and an associate with Alberto's misdeeds. He looked on him as a reckless little adventurer. At that time my father did not have a clear-cut opinion of the Communists. He could not believe there were new conspirators in the rising generation, and if he had suspected that there were any he would have thought them mad. According to him there was nothing, absolutely nothing, to be done against Fascism.

As for my mother, she had an optimistic nature and enjoyed a good piece of drama. She expected someone, someday, somehow, would knock down Mussolini. She would go out in the morning saying, 'I am going to see if Fascism is still on its feet. I am going to see if they have knocked Mussolini down.' She picked up allusions and views in the shops, and turned them into comforting omens. At dinner she would say, 'There is great discontent everywhere. People cannot take any more.'

'Who told you that?' shouted my father.

'My greengrocer told me.'

My father snorted disdainfully.

Every week Paola Carrara received the *Zurnal de Zenève* (that was the way she pronounced French). She had a sister, Gina, in Geneva, and her brother-in-law, Guglielmo Ferrero.[20] Both had gone abroad many years before for political reasons. Paola went occasionally to Geneva, but sometimes her passport would be taken away, and then of course she could not go to see Gina. Presently her passport would be returned and then she could go. She came back after a few months full of hope and encouraging news.

'Listen, this is what Guglielmo told me. This is what Gina said.'

When my mother wanted to bolster her optimism she went to see Paola Carrara. Sometimes, however, she found her in her little sitting-room, full of pearls and dolls and postcards, in the half dark, and in a frantic state. Either they had taken her passport away or the *Zurnal de Zenève* had not arrived and she suspected that it had been confiscated at the frontier.

Mario left his job at Genoa, came to some understanding with Adriano, and was taken into Olivetti's firm. At heart my father was pleased. But before being pleased about it he was angry because he was afraid that Mario had been taken on because he was Adriano's brother-in-law, and not on his own merits.

Paola now had a house in Milan. She had learned to drive a car and went to and fro between Milan, Turin and Ivrea. My father disapproved of this because he thought she never stayed in one place. But none of the Olivettis ever stayed in one place, they were always in their cars, and my father disapproved.

So Mario went to live at Ivrea; he took a room there, and spent his evenings with Gino discussing problems concerning the factory. His relationship with Gino had always been rather cold, but now they became firm friends. Nevertheless Mario was bored to death at Ivrea. During the summer he had been to Paris. He had gone to see Rosselli, and had asked to be put in touch with the 'Justice and Liberty' group in Turin. He had decided quite suddenly to become a conspirator.

Mario came to Turin on Saturdays. He was the same as ever — mysterious, meticulous about hanging his clothes in the wardrobe, and putting his pyjamas and silk shirts in the drawer. He only stayed a short while in the house, put on his raincoat with a resolute businesslike air, went out, and we saw no more of him.

One day my father met him in the Corso Re Umberto with a man whom he knew by sight, called Ginzburg.

'What is Mario up to with that man Ginzburg?'

'What has Mario got to do with Ginzburg?' he asked my mother. Some time before she had begun to learn Russian, 'so as not to get bored'. She and Frances were having lessons from Ginzburg's sister. 'He is a very cultivated, intelligent man, who does very fine translations from Russian.'

'But he is very ugly,' said my father. 'We know Jews are all ugly.'

'And what about you?' said my mother. 'Aren't you a Jew?'

'Well, yes, I am ugly too,' said my father.

Relations between Mario and Alberto were still cold. They no longer had bouts of wild and furious quarrelling, but they still never exchanged a word. They took no notice of each other if they met in the passage, and Mario curled his lips in disdain if Alberto was mentioned to him.

Mario, however, knew Alberto's friend Vittorio, and Mario and Alberto happened to meet face to face in the Corso with Ginzburg and Vittorio, who knew each other well, and Mario happened to ask them both, Ginzburg and Vittorio, to the house for tea. The day they came my mother was very happy because she saw Alberto and Mario together and saw that they had the same friends. It was like being back in the days of Via Pastrengo when Gino's friends used to come and the house was always full of people.

In addition to taking Russian lessons my mother also took piano lessons. She had her piano lessons with a teacher who had been recommended to her by someone called Signora Donati, who had also taken up the piano at a mature age. This lady was tall, big and handsome, with white hair. She was also studying painting in Casorati's studio. In fact she liked painting better than the piano. She

79

idolized painting, Casorati, his studio, his wife and his little boy, and also his house where she was occasionally asked to dinner. She was keen to persuade my mother to take lessons from Casorati too. My mother, however, stood out against this. Signora Donati telephoned her every day and described how much fun she had had painting. She would say to my mother, 'But you have a sense of colour?'

'Yes,' said my mother, 'I think I have a sense of colour.'

'And volume? Do you have any sense of volume?'

'No, I have no sense of volume,' my mother replied.

'You have no sense of volume?'

'No.'

'But colour! You have sense of colour!'

Now that there was more money in the house, my mother had some dresses made. This was a constant activity in addition to Russian and the piano, and really a means of 'not getting bored', because afterwards she did not know when to wear these dresses as she never felt like visiting anyone except Frances and Paola Carrara, and to them she could go in what she was wearing at home. She had her dresses made sometimes 'at Signor Belom's'. He was an old tailor who in his younger days had been my grandmother's suitor in Pisa, when she was looking for a husband and refused to take 'Virginia's leavings'. Or she had them made at home by a dressmaker called Tersilla. Rina no longer came to us, having disappeared into the mists of time, but when my father met Tersilla in the passage he lost his temper, as he used to do when he saw Rina. Tersilla, however, had more spirit than Rina and used to say hello as she went past him with her scissors stuck in her belt, and a polite smile on her small rosy Piedmontese face. My father answered her with a cold nod.

'Tersilla is here. How come she is here again today?' my father shouted to my mother.

'She has come to turn an old coat of mine. One of Signor Belom's coats.'

When he heard the name Belom my father was pacified. He had a high opinion of him because he had been his mother's suitor. He did not know, however, that Signor Belom was one of the most expensive tailors in Turin.

My mother swung backwards and forwards between Signor Belom and Tersilla. When she had a dress made by Belom she would find that it was not so very well cut, and 'fitted badly on the shoulders'. Then afterwards she called in Tersilla, and made her undo it, take it apart, and start again from scratch. 'I shall not go to Signor Belom any more. I shall have everything made by Tersilla,' she declared as she tried on the dress in front of the looking-glass after one of these remakings. There were, however, clothes which never fitted and were 'never quite right', so she gave them to Natalina. So Natalina now had a large quantity of clothes as well. She went out on Sundays in one of Belom's coats which was black and buttoned all the way down the front so that she looked like a parish priest.

Paola also had a lot of clothes made. However, she was always at odds with my mother. She said that my mother's clothes were all wrong and that she had so many made exactly the same, and that she would get Tersilla to copy one of Belom's creations a hundred times over, until one was sick of them. But my mother liked things that way. She said that when we were little children she always had a number of pinafores made for us, all exactly the same, and now, like her children, she wished to have plenty of pinafores for summer and winter. This idea of treating clothes as pinafores did not convince Paola.

When Paola came from Milan in a new dress my mother embraced her and said, 'I do love to see my children in new dresses.' But she immediately felt like having something new made too; not the same because she always thought Paola's clothes too complicated. She had it made 'more pinafore style'. The same thing happened with me. When she ordered a new dress for me, she immediately felt like having one made too. However, she did not admit this to me or to Paola because we used to say that she ordered too many dresses. She would put the material away, neatly folded, in a drawer, until one morning we would see it in Tersilla's hands.

She liked having Tersilla in the house because she enjoyed her company too. 'Lydia, Lydia! Where are you?' my father would bellow when he came home. My mother would be in the ironing-room chatting with Natalina and Tersilla.

'You are always with the servants! Tersilla here again today?' he shouted.

'What can Mario be up to with that Russian all the time?' he asked from time to time. 'A rising star,' he said when he had met his son with Ginzburg on the Corso. However, he saw Ginzburg in a better light and was not over-suspicious of him after he had met him and

Salvatorelli on one occasion in Paola Carrara's sitting-room. He still did not understand what Mario had in common with him.

'What can he be up to with that man Ginzburg?' he asked. 'What the devil can they say to each other? He is ugly,' he said to my mother, meaning Ginzburg, 'because he is a Sephardic Jew. I am an Ashkenazy and that is why I am less ugly.'

He always spoke rather favourably of the Ashkenazic Jews. Adriano on the other hand always praised people of mixed blood, who were he said the best people. Among these he liked best the children of a Jewish father and a Protestant mother, as he was himself.

In those days we had a game at home which Paola had invented and which she and Mario particularly used to play; sometimes my mother joined in. The game consisted of dividing the people we knew into animal, vegetable and mineral. Adriano was a mineral-vegetable and Paola an animal-vegetable. Gino was a mineral-vegetable. Rasetti, whom anyway we had not seen for many years, was pure mineral, and so was Frances. My father was animal-vegetable and so was my mother.

'Twaddle!' said my father, catching a few words in the passage. 'Always that twaddle of yours!'

There were very few vegetables in the world — people of pure imagination; probably only a few great poets had been pure vegetable. Search as we might we could not find a single vegetable among our acquaintances.

Paola said that this game was her own invention. But someone told her later that a classification of this sort had been made by Dante in *De Vulgari Eloquentia*. I do not know whether this is true.

Alberto went to do his military service at Cuneo, and so now Vittorio walked along the Corso alone, since he had already done his service.

ONE SATURDAY Mario did not arrive as usual from Ivrea, nor did he appear on Sunday. My mother was not anxious, however, as there had been previous occasions when he had not come. She supposed that he had gone to Switzerland to see his girl friend — the one who was so thin.

On Monday morning Gino and Piera came to tell us that Mario and a friend had been arrested at Ponte Tresa on the Swiss frontier. Nothing else was known. Gino had had this news from someone in the Olivetti office in Lugano.

My father was not in Turin that day. He came home the following morning. My mother had scarcely had time to inform him of what had happened before the house was full of detectives who had come to make a search.

They found nothing. On the previous day, with Gino's help, we had gone through Mario's drawers in case there was anything there that ought to be burnt. We found nothing except all his shirts — 'his little wardrobe' as Aunt Drusilla used to say.

The detectives went away taking my father with them to the police station. By the evening my father had not returned and we realized that he had been put in prison.

Gino had been arrested at Ivrea after his return there, and was later transferred to the prison in Turin.

Then Adriano came to tell us that when Mario and his friend were going through Ponte Tresa in the car they had been stopped by customs officers looking for cigarettes. They had searched the car and found some anti-Fascist pamphlets. Mario and his friend were made to get out, and the officers started to escort them along the riverside to the police-post. Suddenly Mario had broken away from his captors. He had plunged into the river fully dressed and had swum towards the Swiss bank. The Swiss guards had then come with a boat to pick him up. So now Mario was in Switzerland, in safety.

Adriano's face wore that expression of mingled happiness and fear in time of danger that it had at the time of Turati's flight. He put a car and a driver at my mother's disposal, but she did not know what to do, or where to go. She kept putting her hands together, saying with a mixture of happiness, admiration and alarm, 'In the water, in his overcoat!'

The friend who had been with Mario at Ponte Tresa and owned the car — for Mario neither owned a car nor could he drive — was called Sion Segre. We had seen him sometimes at home with Alberto and Vittorio. He was a fair-haired youth, rather round-shouldered, with a gentle indolent manner. He was a friend of Alberto and Vittorio but we did not know that he knew Mario too. Paola, however, who drove over from Milan immediately, told us that Mario had confided in her. Mario and Sion Segre had already made a number of trips together between Italy and Switzerland with those pamphlets, and everything had always gone smoothly, so they had become increasingly venturesome and loaded the car with more and more pamphlets and newspapers, neglecting every rule of caution. When he plunged into the river one of the guards had drawn his revolver, but the other one had called to him not to shoot, and so Mario owed his life to that guard. The river was turbulent, but Mario was a good swimmer, and was used to icy water because in fact as my mother remembered, during one of his cruises he had swum in the North Sea with the ship's cook. The other passengers had watched him from the deck and applauded, and when they learned that he was an Italian they began to shout '*Viva Mussolini!*'

Nevertheless, he nearly ran out of strength in the river Tresa, hampered as he was by his clothing, and perhaps because of the tension, but by then the Swiss guards had sent the boat to pick him up.

My mother put her hands together and said, 'I wonder if that skinny girl friend of his will give him something to eat.'

Sion Segre was now in prison in Turin, and one of his brothers had also been arrested. Ginzburg had been arrested too, and a number of people who had been associated with Mario in Turin. Vittorio had not been arrested. He was quite nonplussed, he told my mother, because he had been constantly with the anti-Fascist conspirators. His long face with its prominent chin was pale, tense and perplexed. He and Alberto, who was home on leave for a few days, walked up and down the Corso Re Umberto.

My mother did not know how to set about providing my father in prison with clean clothing and things to eat. She told me to look in the telephone directory for Segre's family. But Segre was an orphan and had no one but the brother who had also been arrested. But she knew that the Segre boys were cousins of Pitigrilli[21] and she told me to ring him up to find out how he himself was coping and whether he would be taking clothes and books to his cousins in prison. He replied that he would come and see us.

Pitigrilli was a novelist. Alberto was a great reader of his books, and when my father found one in the house, it was as though he had seen a snake. 'Lydia, Lydia, hide that book at once!' he shouted. The fact was that he was afraid I might read it, Pitigrilli's novels not being thought at all 'suitable' for me. Pitigrilli also edited a review called *Grandi Firme*, and that too was always to be found in Alberto's room in large binders beside his medical books on the shelf.

So Pitigrilli came to see us. He was tall and big. He had long salt and pepper sideburns, and a pale overcoat which he did not take off while he sat solemnly in an armchair and talked to my mother in stern tones with an air of studied concern. He had been in prison once, years ago, and he explained everything to us: the food one could send on certain days of the week to the prisoner, and how one had to shell nuts at home, and peel apples and oranges and cut the bread into thin slices, since knives were not allowed in prison. He explained everything, and then stayed on and talked elegantly to my mother, his legs crossed, his big overcoat unbuttoned, and knitting his bushy eyebrows. My mother told him that I wrote stories and wanted me to show him an exercise-book in which I had made careful fair copies of the three or four stories I had written. Pitigrilli leafed through it for a while with that mysterious, arrogant, sad air of his.

Then Alberto and Vittorio came in and were each introduced to him. And Pitigrilli went out on to the Corso with one of them on either side, walking ponderously, with his arrogant, sad air and his voluminous overcoat over his shoulders.

My father remained in prison for a fortnight or three weeks, I think, and Gino for two months. My mother went to the prison in the morning on the days when one was allowed to send in food, with a bundle of clean clothes and packets of peeled oranges and shelled nuts.

Then she went to the police-station. Sometimes she was received by a man called Finucci, sometimes by a man called Lutri. These two

85

characters seemed to her to be very powerful and to hold the future of our family in their hands. 'Today it was Finucci,' she would say on her return; she was quite happy because he had reassured her and said that there was no charge against her husband or Gino and that they would shortly be released. 'Today it was Lutri,' she would say, happy just the same because though his manner was rough, she thought he was perhaps more sincere. She also felt flattered by the fact that both these characters spoke of all of us by name, and seemed to know us all thoroughly. They spoke of 'Mario', 'Gino', 'Piera' and 'Paola'. They referred to my father as 'the professor', and when my mother explained to them that he was a scientist, and had never had anything to do with politics, and only thought about tissue cells, they nodded and told her not to worry. Little by little, however, she began to be frightened because my father did not come home, nor Gino either, and then one day an article appeared in the newspaper, headlined 'Group of anti-Fascists discovered in Turin ganging up with Paris exiles'. 'Ganging up' my mother repeated in distress. This phrase sounded full of dark threats. She wept in the sitting-room with her friends round her — Paola Carrara, Frances, Signora Donati, and all the women younger than herself whom she used to protect and help and comfort when they had no money or their husbands yelled at them. Now it was their turn to help and comfort her. Paola Carrara said that a letter should be sent to the *Zurnal de Zenève*.

'I wrote at once to Gina,' she said. 'You will see now, there will be a protest in the *Zurnal de Zenève*.'

'It is like the Dreyfus affair,' my mother kept on repeating. 'It is like the Dreyfus affair.'

There was constant coming and going at the house, what with Paola, Adriano, Terni who had come up from Florence specially, and Frances and Paola Carrara. Piera, who was in mourning for her own father and also expecting a baby, had come to live with us. Natalina ran to and fro between the kitchen and the sitting-room with cups of coffee. She was excited and happy. She was always happy when there was turmoil — people in the house, noise, days of drama, bells ringing and lots of beds to make.

Then my mother left with Adriano for Rome. Adriano had discovered that there was in Rome someone called Dr Veratti who was Mussolini's personal doctor. He was an anti-Fascist and prepared to help other anti-Fascists. It was, however, difficult to gain access to him, but Adriano had found two men who knew him, Ambrosini and Silvestri, and through them he hoped to get in touch with the doctor.

Piera and I remained alone with Natalina in the house. One night we were woken up by a ring at the door. We got up, alarmed. Two soldiers had come to look for Alberto who was now an officer cadet at Cuneo. He had not returned to barracks, and it was not known where he was.

He could be court-martialled, Piera said, for desertion. We racked our brains all night as to where he could have got to. Piera thought that he might have taken fright and escaped to France. But the next day Vittorio told us that he had merely gone to meet a girl in the mountains and had spent the time with her, skiing peacefully, forgetting to return to barracks. He had now returned to Cuneo and was under arrest there.

My mother returned from Rome more frightened than ever. Yet she had managed to enjoy herself in Rome because she always enjoyed travelling. She and Adriano had stayed with someone called Signora Bondi, a cousin of my father's, and had tried to get in contact with Margherita as well as with Dr Veratti. Margherita was one of the many Margheritas and Reginas among my father's relations, and this Margherita was famous because she was a friend of Mussolini. However, my father and mother had not seen her for many years. My mother had not been able to meet her since she was not in Rome at that time, nor had she succeeded in speaking to Dr Veratti. But Silvestri and Ambrosini had given them some hope, and Adriano had another source — he was always saying 'one of my sources' — who had told them that both my father and Gino would very soon be freed. Among the persons arrested the only ones who were really compromised, and they said would be tried, were Sion Segre and Ginzburg. 'It's like the Dreyfus affair,' my mother kept repeating.

Then one evening my father came home. He had no tie, or laces in his shoes, for they had taken them away in prison. He had a bundle of dirty linen under his arm, wrapped in a sheet of newspaper, and a long beard, and was very pleased with himself for having been in prison.

Gino, however, remained inside for another two months. One day when my mother and Piera's mother were taking some clothes and food to the prison in a taxi, the taxi happened to collide with another car. Neither my mother nor Piera's mother was hurt at all, but there they were, sitting in this smashed up taxi, with their parcels on their knees, with the driver swearing, and a crowd all round them, including some guards, for they were only a few yards from the prison. My mother's only fear was that people would realize that they were taking those parcels to the prison, and would think that they were the relatives of some murderer! When Adriano was told this story, he said there was certainly something bad in my mother's stars and that was why she had so many dangerous adventures at that time.

Finally Gino was released as well, and my mother said: 'So now it is back to the ordinary boring life.'

My father was furious when he learnt that Alberto was under arrest and in danger of being court-martialled. 'That scoundrel! While his family was inside he went off to ski with a girl!'

'I am worried about Alberto,' my father said and woke up in the night. 'It will be no joke at all if he is court-martialled. I am very worried about Mario. What is he going to do?'

He was, however, happy to have a son who was a conspirator. He had not expected it and had never thought of Mario as an anti-Fascist. When they had arguments Mario would always contradict him, and would disparage the Socialists of former days who were dear to his parents. He used to say that Turati was completely gullible and had piled one mistake upon another. My father used to say as much himself, but when he heard Mario say so he was deeply offended. 'He is a Fascist,' he would say to my mother at times. 'At heart he is a Fascist.'

Now he could not say that any more: Mario had become a famous political exile. All the same my father was displeased that his arrest and escape had occurred while he was employed in Olivetti's factory, since he feared that he might have compromised the factory, Adriano and old Olivetti.

'I said that he ought not to go into Olivetti's,' he shouted at my mother, 'and now he has compromised the factory. How good Adriano is! He has done so much for me. He is very good. All the Olivettis are good.'

Through one or other of the Olivetti offices Paola received a letter in Mario's notorious handwriting, which was very small and almost illegible. A note read: 'To my vegetable and mineral friends. I am well and not in need of anything.'

Sion Segre and Ginzburg were tried before the Political Court Special Tribunal, and were condemned to one year and two years imprisonment respectively. The sentences were halved later, through an amnesty. Ginzburg was sent to the penitentiary at Civitavecchia.

Alberto was not court-martialled and came home after his military service. He resumed his walks on the Corso with Vittorio. Through force of habit my father shouted once again 'Scoundrel' and 'Rascal', when he heard him come in, at whatever time of day it might be.

My mother resumed her piano lessons. Her teacher, a man with a little black moustache, was terrified of my father, and crept along the passage on tiptoe with his sheets of music.

'I cannot bear your piano teacher,' my father shouted, 'he looks very dubious.' 'Oh no, Beppino, he is a good man. He is very good to his little girl. He is very kind, and teaches her Latin. He is poor.'

My mother had given up Russian. She could no longer have lessons from Ginzburg's sister as that would have been compromising.

New phrases had been added to our family vocabulary. 'You cannot invite Salvatorelli: it is compromising. You cannot have that book in the house: it could be compromising. There may be a search.' Paola said that the main entrance to our building was 'under observation', and that there was always a fellow in a raincoat hanging about there, and she thought that whenever she went out she was being followed.

Anyhow, 'ordinary boring life' didn't last long. A year later the police came to arrest Alberto, and we heard that they had arrested Vittorio again, and a good many other people as well. They came early in the morning. It was perhaps six o'clock. The search began, and Alberto stood there in his pyjamas between two policemen while three others rummaged among his medical books, the *Grandi Firme* and the thrillers.

The police gave me permission to go to school, and at the door my mother slipped into my satchel envelopes with her bills because she was afraid that in the course of the search they might be seen by my father and he would scold her for spending too much.

'Alberto! They have put Alberto inside! But he has never had anything to do with politics,' my mother said, quite overcome.

'They have put him inside,' said my father, 'because he is Mario's brother, and my son. You don't think it's for anything he has done himself, do you?'

My mother resumed her visits to the prison with clean clothes, and there she met Vittorio's parents and other prisoners' relations.

'Such respectable people!' she said of Vittorio's parents. 'Such a respectable family! And they told me that Vittorio is doing terribly well. He had just passed his solicitor's examination very successfully. Alberto has always chosen very good friends.'

'Carlo Levi[22] is inside too!' she said with a mixture of pride and relief. For one thing, she was frightened that so many of them were inside and that a big trial might be coming up. Yet she was at the same time relieved that so many of them were inside, and she was flattered to know that Alberto was there with respectable, famous, mature people.

'Professor Giua is inside as well.'

'Anyway I don't like Carlo Levi's pictures,' said my father, who never missed an opportunity of declaring that he did not like Carlo Levi's work.

'Oh no, Beppino, I think they are lovely,' said my mother. 'The portrait of his mother is beautiful. You have not seen it.'

'Dishwater!' said my father. 'I cannot bear modern painting.'

'H'mph! They will let Giua out straight away,' he said. 'He is not compromised.'

My father could never understand which were the real conspirators. Actually we heard after a few days that they had found in Giua's house letters written in invisible ink and of them all he was the one in the greatest danger.

'Invisible ink!' exclaimed my father. 'Well of course, he is a chemist and he knows how to make invisible ink!'

He was thoroughly amazed and perhaps vaguely jealous; this Giua whom he used to meet at Paola Carrara's had always seemed to him a quiet, well-balanced, thoughtful man. And now he had leapt at one bound to the centre of this political business. Vittorio too was said to be in an extremely dangerous situation. 'Gossip!' my father said, 'all gossip. No one knows anything.'

Giulio Einaudi[23] and Pavese[24] had also been arrested. These were men whom my father hardly knew, or perhaps only by name. But like his wife he felt flattered that Alberto should be with people like that.

90

When they discovered he was mixed up with this group, which they knew published a review called *La Cultura*, they felt that Alberto had suddenly become a worthwhile member of society. 'They have put him inside with the "cultural people". He only ever reads *Grandi Firme*!'

'He was to have taken his examination in comparative biology. He will never do that now. He will never take his degree,' he said to my mother that night.

Alberto, Vittorio and the others were now taken on a troop train in handcuffs to Rome and put in Regina Coeli prison. My mother tried once again going to the police-station. But Finucci and Lutri said that the affair had now become the responsibility of headquarters in Rome, and they knew nothing about it.

Adriano had learned from his source that all telephone calls between Alberto and Vittorio had been recorded. Alberto and Vittorio in fact endlessly rang each other up in the rare intervals when they were not together, walking on the Corso.

'Those stupid telephone calls,' said my mother. 'Fancy recording them one by one!'

She did not know what they had said to each other in those calls, because Alberto always spoke in a whisper on the telephone. However, she was convinced that he was always talking about nothing in particular, and my father was of the same opinion. 'Alberto is so mindless,' he said. 'Fancy putting inside someone who is mindlessness personified.'

They began to talk once more of Dr Veratti and Margherita. But my father would not hear Margherita's name mentioned. 'Do you think I am going to see Margherita? I shall not go. I wouldn't dream of it.'

Years before this Margherita had written a life of Mussolini, and the fact that he had a biographer of Mussolini among his cousins seemed to my father outrageous. 'Besides, she would not receive me. Do you think I am going to go asking Margherita for favours?'

My father went to police headquarters in Rome to try and get some news. But as he was absolutely devoid of any sense of diplomacy, and bellowed as usual in his deep loud voice, I do not think he succeeded in obtaining anything or achieving much in the way of meetings or information. He had been received by someone who had told him his name was De Stefani. But as my father always got names wrong when he spoke to my mother afterwards he called him 'Di Stefano'; he described what he was like.

'But that is not Di Stefano, Beppino,' she said. 'That is Anchise. I was there myself last year.'

'What do you mean, Anchise? He told me his name is Di Stefano. He can't have told me wrong.'

My father and mother argued about Di Stefano and Anchise every time he was mentioned and my father continued to call the man Di Stefano, although according to my mother he was Anchise beyond all possible doubt.

Alberto wrote from Rome that he was sorry not to be able to see the city. He had as a matter of fact only seen Rome for half an hour at the age of three. On one occasion he wrote that he had washed his hair in milk, and that afterwards his hair stank and the whole cell stank. The Director of Prisons held up this letter, and told him that he should write less nonsense in his letters.

Alberto was sent into forced residence in a place called Ferrandina in Lucania. As for Giua and Vittorio, they were tried and got fifteen years each.

'If Mario came back to Italy,' my father said, 'he would get fifteen years. Twenty years!'

MARIO now wrote from Paris in his minute illegible handwriting. His letters were short and concise and my parents had difficulty deciphering them.

They went to see him. In Paris he was living in a garret and still wearing the clothes in which he had plunged into the water at Ponte Tresa, which were now faded and worn. My mother wanted to buy him a suit, but he refused to give up these faded garments. He at once asked for news of Sion Segre and Ginzburg who were still in prison, and spoke very highly of Ginzburg, but as of someone who was far away, someone who had not been ousted from his thoughts or affections but had been rather laid aside. As for his own adventures and escape he appeared to have forgotten about them completely.

He did his own washing, but he only possessed two worn-out shirts. He washed his clothes with great care and with the same meticulous attention with which he had once looked after his silk underclothes and put them away in a drawer. He swept his attic himself with meticulous care. He was always well shaved, clean and spruce despite his worn-out clothes, and according to my mother he looked more than ever like a Chinese. He had a cat. In a corner of the attic was a box full of sawdust. The cat was very clean, said Mario, and never made a mess on the floor. My father said Mario had a fixation with this cat. He got up early in the morning to go and buy milk for it. Like my grandmother my father could not bear cats, and my mother didn't much like them either; she preferred dogs.

'Why don't you have a dog instead?' she asked.

'What! a dog!' shouted my father. 'If he kept a dog that would be the last straw.'

In Paris Mario had broken away from the 'Justice and Liberty' groups. He kept up with them for a time and did some work for their paper. Then he realized that he did not much like them.

Mario was the one who as a small boy had made up the rhyme about the Tosi boys with whom he did not like playing: 'Nothing in this world annoys/Or plagues us like the Tosi boys.'

Now the 'Justice and Liberty' groups had taken the place of the

Tosi boys for him. Everything they thought, said or wrote, irritated him. He did nothing but find fault with them and said: 'Amid the bitter sorbs/It is not natural the sweet fig should fruit.' (Dante, *Inferno* XV 64).

He was the sweet fig and the bitter sorbs were the 'Justice and Liberty' people.

'It is quite true,' he said, 'quite true, "Amid the bitter sorbs it is not natural the sweet fig should fruit." '

He would laugh as he said this and stroke his jaw as in the old days he used to say '*Il baco del calo del malo*'.

Mario had begun to read Dante, and had discovered that he was a marvellous poet. He had also taken up Greek and was reading Herodotus and Homer.

But he could not stand Pascoli[25] or Carducci.[26] Carducci drove him mad. 'He was a monarchist. First he was a republican, and then he became a monarchist because he fell in love with that silly woman Queen Margherita. And to think that he lived at the same time as Baudelaire, the same century. Leopardi,[27] now there was a great poet. The only modern poets are Leopardi and Baudelaire. It is absurd that they still read Carducci in Italian schools.'

My father and mother went to visit the Louvre, and Mario asked them if they had seen the Poussins.

No, they had not looked at Poussins. There were so many other things to see. 'What!' said Mario, 'You did not see the Poussins. There was no point in going to the Louvre, then. The only pictures worth seeing in the Louvre are the Poussins.'

'This Poussin,' said my mother. 'It is the first time I have heard of him.'

Mario had made friends in Paris with a man called Cafi. He could talk of nobody else. 'A new star rising,' said my father. Cafi was half Russian and half Italian. He had emigrated to Paris many years before and was extremely poor and in bad health. He had written sheafs of pages which he gave to his friends to read, but he never did anything about getting them printed. He said that when one has written something there is no need to have it printed: to have written and read it to friends is enough. There is no need to preserve it for posterity because posterity does not count for anything. Mario could not explain very well what was written on all those pages. Everything was in those pages, everything.

94

Cafi did not eat. He lived on nothing, on half a potato. His clothes were in rags and his shoes were broken. If ever he did have a little money he spent it on fancy food and champagne.

'Mario is so intolerant!' said my father to my mother. 'He finds fault with everything. He cannot agree with anyone — only with that man Cafi.'

'He seems to have discovered that Carducci is a bore. I have known that for years,' said my mother.

They were both offended because Mario did not seem to miss Italy. He was in love with France and with Paris especially, and endlessly used French words when he talked. He sneered disdainfully when he spoke about Italy. My parents had never been nationalistic. In fact they hated nationalism in all its guises. But this disdain for Italy seemed to include themselves and all of us and our family life.

Then my father was displeased because Mario had broken with the 'Justice and Liberty' groups. The head of these groups was Carlo Rosselli, who had given Mario money and put him up when he first arrived in Paris. My parents had known the Rossellis for many years and were friends with Carlo's mother, Signora Amelia, who lived in Florence.

'Mind you are not rude to Rosselli,' my father said to Mario.

Mario had two other friends besides Cafi. One was Renzo Giua, the son of the Giua who was in prison. He was a pale youth with smouldering eyes and slicked back hair. He had escaped from Italy alone, over the Alps. The other was Chiaromonte, whom my mother had met years before at Paola's house one summer at Forte dei Marmi. Chiaromonte was big and solid, with curly black hair. Both these friends of Mario had broken with 'Justice and Liberty', and both were friends of Cafi and spent their days listening to him when he read from his pencil-written pages, which would never be published because he despised printed books.

Chiaromonte had a wife who was very ill, and he was very poor. Yet he helped Cafi when he could. Mario helped him too. They lived like that in close friendship, sharing the little they had, without attaching themselves to any group, or making plans for the future because no future was possible. They expected war to break out and the stupid would win it, because, Mario said, the stupid always win.

'That man Cafi,' my father said to his wife, 'must be an anarchist. Mario is an anarchist too. He has always been an anarchist at heart.'

From Paris my parents went on to Brussels, where there was a conference on biology. They found Terni there and other friends of my father, and his pupils and assistants. My father felt relieved; being with Mario wore him out. 'He always contradicts me. As soon as I open my mouth he contradicts me.'

My father very much enjoyed travelling from time to time when there was a conference. He liked meeting biologists and having discussions with them, while he scratched his head and his back. And he enjoyed dragging my mother, at a terrible pace without ever letting her stop, round galleries and museums. He liked staying in hotels too. But he always woke very early in the morning and always felt hungry when he woke up. Until he had had some breakfast he was in a ferocious mood. He paced up and down the room, and looked out of the window for the first signs of dawn. When at last it was five o'clock, he attacked the telephone and ordered breakfast with a shout, '*Deux thés. Deux thés complets! Avec de l'eau chaude!*'

As a rule they forgot to bring him *l'eau chaude* or any jam because at that time of day the waiters were still sleepy. Finally he fell on his breakfast of jam and brioches and then made my mother get up, saying 'Lydia, let us go, it is late. Let us go and see the town.'

'What an ass that Mario is,' he would say from time to time. 'He has always been an ass and he has always been intolerant. I shall be annoyed if he is rude to Rosselli.'

'He is always with that man Cafi. Cafi! Cafi!' my mother said when they were home again and she was telling Paola and me about Mario. She said 'with Cafi' as once she used to say 'with Pajetta' when she complained about Alberto, and she asked Paola about Poussin. 'Is this Poussin really so very good?'

Paola went to see Mario too. They quarrelled and no longer got on. They no longer played their game of vegetable and mineral. They could not agree about anything and had opposite opinions. Paola bought a dress in Paris. Mario had always considered her very smart, and used to praise her dresses and her taste. It had been usual for Paola to express her opinions and for Mario to accept them. But now Mario did not like the dress she had bought in Paris. He said it made her look like a 'magistrate's wife'. Paola was offended. Then Chiaromonte whom she used to see in the past when they were on holiday at the seaside, at Forte dei Marmi, no longer appealed to her.

But she no longer recognized the Chiaromonte who used to take her rowing and swimming, flirted with her friends, joked about everything and went dancing at night at the Capannina, in this new character as a political exile, with no money and his wife so ill, and such friends with Cafi.

Mario told her she was bourgeois and Paola said, 'Yes, I am bourgeois and it does not matter to me at all.'

She went to see Proust's grave. Mario had never been. 'Proust no longer means anything to him,' she told my mother on her return. 'He does not even remember him. He only likes Herodotus.'

Seeing that Mario had no raincoat she bought him a good one and he immediately gave it to Cafi. He said that Cafi should not get wet when it rained because he had heart trouble.

'Cafi! Cafi! Cafi!' Paola said disgustedly as well; and she agreed with my father that Mario was very wrong to move away from Rosselli's group, and that those two — Mario and Chiaromonte — were quite isolated in Paris and had completely lost touch with reality.

ALBERTO had returned from restricted residence, had taken his degree and had married. Contrary to all my father's predictions he had become a doctor and had started to treat patients. He had a consulting room now and became angry with his wife Miranda if the room was not tidy or if there were newspapers lying around. He got angry if there were no ashtrays: he was a chain-smoker but he no longer threw his butt-ends on the floor. Patients came to see him and he examined them, while they told him about themselves. He listened because he liked hearing about people's lives.

After that in his white coat with his stethoscope dangling from his neck he would go into the next room where Miranda would be stretched on a sofa with a hot-water bottle, wrapped in a rug, for she was a chilly person and lazy. He had coffee made for himself.

Alberto was always restless, just as he had been as a boy. He drank coffee continually, and smoked continually, in little puffs without inhaling, as though he were drinking cigarettes.

His friends came to see him and he took their blood pressures and gave them samples of medicines. He found something wrong with each of them. But he could find nothing wrong with his wife. She would say: 'Do give me a tonic. I must be ill. I always have a headache. I am so tired.' But he would say, 'You aren't ill: it is just that you are made of second-rate materials.'

Miranda was small, thin and fair-haired with blue eyes. She would stay indoors for hours and hours, wearing one of Alberto's dressing-gowns and wrapped in the rug.

'I really think I ought to go to Ospedaletti,' she would say, 'to Elena's.'

She always dreamed of going to Ospedaletti where her sister Elena used to spend the winter. Her sister was fair as well, and resembled Miranda but she was rather more energetic. At that moment she would be lying in the sun on a deck-chair, wearing dark glasses and with a rug over her legs. Or she might be playing bridge.

Miranda and her sister were good bridge-players, and had won tournaments. Miranda's house was full of ashtrays which she had won at bridge. When she was playing bridge Miranda shook off her lethargy. Bending her little tilted nose over the cards, her face took on a cunning, cheerful expression, while her eyes sparkled.

Generally, however, she could not be parted from her armchair and rug. Towards evening she got up, went into the kitchen and looked inside a saucepan where there was a chicken cooking. Alberto would ask: 'Why do we always eat boiled chicken in this house?'

Alberto also played bridge, but he always lost.

Miranda knew all about the Stock Exchange as her father was a stockbroker. 'You know,' she would say to my mother, 'I am thinking of selling my Incet. You ought to sell your property shares. Why are you waiting?'

My mother went to my father: 'You should sell property shares. Miranda says so.'

My father said, 'Miranda. What do you think Miranda knows?' However, when he saw Miranda he said, 'You understand the Stock Exchange. Do you think I should sell property shares?'

Then later he would say to my mother, 'What a stupid creature that Miranda is. She has lots of headaches but she does understand the Stock Exchange. She has a lot of flair for business.'

When Alberto announced that he was getting married, my father made a great scene: then he became resigned. Yet he woke up in the night and said: 'How will they get by? They haven't a penny, and Miranda is a stupid creature.'

It was true they had not much money. But soon Alberto began to earn. Nice little women came to him to be examined and to tell him about their aches and pains. He listened with close attention: he was endowed with curiosity and patience. He delighted in hearing about people's aches and pains and illnesses. Now he only read medical journals. He did not read Pitigrilli novels any more. He had in fact read them all and Pitigrilli had not written any new ones. He had disappeared and no one knew where he was.

Alberto no longer strolled along the Corso Re Umberto. His friend Vittorio was in prison, and the only news he had of him was when Vittorio's parents had bronchitis and sent for him.

Alberto had his suits made by a tailor called Vittorio Foa. One day while the tailor was fitting him he said, 'I come to you because of your name.' The tailor was pleased and thanked him. In fact Vittorio's name was Foa, like the tailor's.

'This stupid bronchitis!' Alberto said to Miranda. 'It is always stupid diseases. I never get a chance to treat some complicated, out of the way disease! I am utterly fed up. It is just not enough fun.'

In fact he enjoyed being a doctor but he was unwilling to admit it.

My mother said: 'Alberto is keen on medicine really.' Or she would say: 'I want to go and see Alberto. I have a slight stomach-ache today.'

'What!' said my father. 'What do you suppose that sausage Alberto knows? You have a stomach-ache because you ate too much yesterday. I will give you a pill.'

Alberto lived near us and my mother went every day to see Miranda. She would find her in an armchair. Alberto would come out of his consulting-room for a moment, in his white coat, his stethoscope round his neck, and warm himself at the radiator. He and his mother both had the same weakness for standing next to a radiator. Miranda was wrapped up in a rug and my mother said, 'Get up, dear. Wash your face in cold water. Let us go for a walk. I'll take you to the cinema.'

But Miranda said, 'I can't. I have to stay in. I am expecting my cousin. Besides I have too much of a headache!'

Then Alberto said, 'Miranda is lifeless. She is lazy. She is made of second-rate materials.'

Miranda was always expecting cousins. She had so many of them, and Alberto would say, 'I am fed up with treating your cousins. Turin is such a boring place. You get so bored here. Nothing ever happens. At least before they used to arrest us. They don't do that any more now. They have forgotten us. I feel forgotten, left in the shade.'

PAOLA had now come to live in Turin too. She lived on the hill, in a large white house with a curving terrace looking out over the Po.

Paola loved the river, the streets, the hill, and the avenues on the Valentino where once she had walked with her short boy friend. She always looked back with affection on those times. But now even Turin had become greyer, sadder, more boring. She found that so many people, so many friends, were far away, in prison. Paola no longer recognized the streets of her girlhood, when she had very few dresses and read Proust.

Now she had a lot of dresses made by dressmakers. She also had Tersilla at home, and she and my mother used to argue about her. Paola said that Tersilla gave her a feeling of security, of the continuity of life.

Occasionally she asked Alberto and Miranda to dinner, and Sion Segre who had been released from prison. Sion Segre had a sister called Ilda who was usually in Palestine with her husband and children, but came to Turin from time to time.

Paola and Ilda had made friends. Ilda was good-looking, tall and fair, and she and Paola used to go for long walks in the town.

Ilda's children were called Ben and Ariel and went to school in Jerusalem. She lived an austere life in Jerusalem and talked exclusively of Jewish problems. But when she came to stay with her brother in Turin she liked talking about clothes and going out.

My mother was always rather jealous of Paola's friends, and when a new one appeared she would be in a bad mood, and feel that she had been put on one side. At such times she got up in the morning grey in the face with puffy eyelids, saying 'I have got a *catramonaccia*.' This was the name she gave to a combination of black depression and loneliness, usually combined with indigestion. When she had a *catramonaccia* she made herself cosy in the sitting-room; she was cold and wrapped herself up in woollen shawls and thought that Paola did not love her any more, did not come to see her but went out with her friends. 'I am fed up,' she said. 'There is

101

nothing to distract me. There is nothing worse than being bored. If only I could be nice and ill.'

Sometimes she caught influenza. She was happy then, because she felt that influenza was a more distinguished illness than her usual bouts of indigestion. She took her temperature: thirty-seven point four.

'Do you know, I am ill?' she said cheerfully to my father. 'It's thirty-seven point four.'

'Thirty-seven point four!' said my father. 'That is not much. I go to the laboratory with thirty-nine.'

My mother said, 'Let us hope that this evening . . .' But she would not wait for the evening; she took her temperature every other minute, 'Still thirty-seven point four. But I do feel ill.'

Paola on her side was also jealous of my mother's friends. Not of Frances or of Paola Carrara, but of the young friends whom my mother protected and helped, and took for walks or to the cinema. Paola would come to see my mother and be told that she had gone out with one of these young friends. Then Paola would lose her temper: 'She is always out. She is never at home!'

She was angry too when my mother passed on Tersilla to one of her young friends: 'You shouldn't have given her Tersiila, I needed her to alter the children's overcoats.'

'Our Mama is too young,' Paola complained to me. 'I should have liked to have had an elderly fat mama, with white hair, who was always at home and embroidered table-cloths. Like Adriano's Mama. It would give me such a sense of security to have a mama who was very old and quiet; one who was not jealous of my friends. Then I should come to see her, and there she would be, at her embroidery, always serene and dressed in black, and she would give me good advice.'

She said to her mother, 'If you're so fed up, why don't you learn to embroider. My mother-in-law spends all her time embroidering.'

'But your mother-in-law is deaf. What can I do if I am not deaf like her. I get tired of being at home all the time. I want to be out and about. Can you see me learning to embroider? I am no good. I don't even know how to darn. When I mend Papa's socks the darning is so awful that Natalina has to do it again.'

She had taken up Russian again, by herself, and practised her words on the sofa; when Paola came to see her she repeated sentences

102

out of the grammar to her, syllable by syllable. Paola said. 'Phew, Mama is such a bore with her Russian.'

Paola was jealous of Miranda and said to my mother, 'You are always going to Miranda. You never come to see me.'

Miranda had had a baby, and they had called him Vittorio. Paola had had a baby girl about the same time. She said that Miranda's child was ugly: 'He has ugly, coarse features,' she said. 'He looks like an engine-driver's son.' When my mother went to see Miranda's baby she would say, 'I am going to see how the engine-driver is.'

But my mother liked all babies. She liked their nurses too. They reminded her of the days when she had her own babies. She had had a collection of nurses, both wet and dry, and they had taught her sons. She would sing around the house and say, 'That was Mario's nurse's song, that was Gino's nurse's.'

Gino's son Arturo was born in the year my father was arrested. With his nurse he came with us on our summer holiday in the country. My mother always chatted with her when she was in the house.

'You are always with the servants,' my father said. 'You use the excuse of going to look at the children, and then you stay to gossip with the servants.'

'But she is such a nice woman, Beppino. She is an anti-Fascist; she thinks as we do.'

'I forbid you to talk politics with the servants.'

Roberto was the only one of his grandchildren that my father liked.

When a new grandson was shown to him he would say, 'Yes, but Roberto looks better!' Roberto, his first grandson, was probably the only one he ever looked at properly.

When holiday time came around my father nearly always rented the same house; for years he never wanted to change. It was a large house of grey stone at Perlotoa near Gressoney, and looked across a field.

Paola's children came with us and Gino's little son. But Alberto's baby, the engine-driver, was taken to Bardonecchia, because Miranda's sister, Elena, had a house there.

My father and mother despised Bardonecchia, though I do not know why. They said there was no sun there, and it was a horrible place. To listen to them you might think it was a cess-pit.

'She is a silly woman, Miranda,' my father said. 'She could have come here. The child would have been much better off here than at Bardonecchia, I am sure.'

'Poor engine-driver,' said my mother.

The child came back from Bardonecchia, where he had had a very nice time. He was a very pretty baby, with fair hair and rosy cheeks. He didn't look in the least like an engine-driver.

'He is all right, you know,' my father said. 'Bardonecchia has not done him any harm.'

Some years we went to Forte dei Marmi because Roberto needed sea air. My father was not keen on the seaside. He sat reading under the beach umbrella in his town clothes. He got cross because he did not like people in bathing-suits. My mother, however, bathed, but as she could not swim she stayed close to the shore. When she was in the water she enjoyed it and let the waves run over her. But when she came back and sat beside my father she too was rather put out. She was jealous of Paola who would go off in a rowing-boat right out to sea, and never seemed to come back.

In the evenings Paola went dancing at the Capannina, and my father said, 'She goes dancing every evening. What an ass she is!'

In the mountains though, at the house in Perlotoa, my father was always happy and so was my mother too. Paola and Piera came only for short visits. My mother had a lovely time with Natalina, the babies and their nurses.

I was bored to death on those holidays. In the house next to ours were Lucio and Frances. Dressed from head to foot in white, they would go to play tennis in the village. Adele Rasetti was there also, at an hotel in the village. She was the same as ever, and just like her son with her thin drawn, greenish face, her eyes as sharp as pinpricks. She collected insects in her handkerchief and put them in a lump of moss on the windowledge.

My mother said, 'I do like Adele.' Her son was now a well known physicist working in Rome with Fermi.[28] 'I always said that Rasetti was very intelligent,' was my father's comment, 'but he is dry, very dry.'

Frances came and sat on a bench in the garden next to my mother. She had a tennis racquet with her and her hair was tied back in a white bandeau. She talked about her sister-in-law in Argentina,

Uncle Mauro's wife, and mimicked the way she said in semi-Spanish 'commo no!'

'Do you remember,' my father said, 'when we were young and we went on a hike with Paola Carrara and she described the crevasses as "those holes you fall into"?'

'Do you remember,' my mother asked, 'when Lucio was a little boy and we had told him that when you are hiking you must never say you are thirsty, and he said "I am thirsty but I am not saying so"?'

'Commo no!' said Frances.

'Lydia, don't pick your cuticles,' my father bellowed. 'It is so ungraceful.'

'Adele for a little and then Frances for a little,' my mother said. 'The days slip by.'

But when Paola came to see her children my mother was restless and discontented. She followed her about everywhere, and watched while she unpacked her various pots of face creams. She had just as many face creams herself, of the same kinds, but she never remembered to put them on.

'Your skin is getting cracked,' said Paola. 'You should take care of it — you should use a good nourishing cream every evening.'

In the mountains my mother wore rough heavy skirts and Paola said: 'You dress too much like a Swiss.' 'These mountains are so depressing,' Paola said. 'I can't bear them.' 'They are all minerals,' she added later when she and I were together, referring to the game we used to play with Mario. 'Adele Rasetti is really pure mineral. I am no longer up to being with such mineral people.'

She went away after a few days and my father said 'Why don't you stay a bit longer? You are a silly ass!'

IN THE autumn I went with my mother on a visit to Mario, who was now teaching in a boarding-school in a small village near Clermont-Ferrand. He had made great friends with the headmaster and his wife. He said they were remarkable people, cultivated and honest, the kind one only found in France.

He had a small room in the school, with a coal stove. From the windows one looked out on a snow-covered landscape. He wrote long letters to Chiaromonte and Cafi in Paris. He was also translating Herodotus. Under his jacket he wore a dark pullover with a rolled collar which the headmaster's wife had made for him. In return he had given her a work-basket.

Everyone knew him and he would stop to talk to people and be taken home to drink *vin blanc*. 'He has become so French,' said my mother.

In the evenings he played cards with the headmaster and his wife, listened to their talk and discussed educational methods with them. They also talked at length about the *soupe* they had had at supper and argued whether there was enough onion in it.

'He has become so patient!' my mother said. 'He is so patient with those people. He was never patient with us when he was at home. He found us boring. But I think those people are more boring than we are,' and then she added, 'He is only patient because they are French.'

At the end of the winter Leone Ginzburg returned to Turin from the penitentiary at Civitavecchia where he had served his sentence. He wore an overcoat that was too short for him and a shabby hat. The hat sat slightly askew on top of his black hair. He walked slowly with his hands in his pockets, and looked anxiously about him with his dark penetrating eyes, his thin lips, knitted brows, and tortoiseshell spectacles sitting rather far down his big nose.

He went to live with his mother and sister in an apartment over by Corso Francia. He was under special surveillance: that is to say, he had to return home as soon as it was dark and the police came to check that he was in. He spent the evenings with Pavese. They had been friends for years. Pavese was in a state of deep depression after an unfortunate love affair. He went to see Leone every evening, hanging up his lilac-coloured scarf and belted overcoat on the hat stand in the hall, and sitting down at the table. Leone sat on the sofa, leaning his elbow against the wall.

Pavese explained that he did not come out of courage or in a spirit of sacrifice. He simply came because otherwise he would not know how to pass the evenings; he could not bear to spend them alone. He said also that he did not come to talk politics, because he did not 'give a damn' about politics. Sometimes he smoked his pipe all evening in silence. Occasionally he sat twisting his hair round his fingers while he talked about himself.

Leone had a limitless capacity for listening, and could listen very attentively to other people's stories even when he was deeply absorbed in thinking about himself.

Presently Leone's sister came in with the tea. She and her mother had taught Pavese to say in Russian, 'I like tea with sugar and lemon'.

At midnight Pavese took his scarf off the hat-stand, wound it tight about his neck, and slipped on his overcoat. He went off down the Corso Francia, tall and pale, with his collar turned up, his empty pipe between his strong white teeth, with rapid strides and his shoulders squared.

Leone stood for a while beside the bookcase, pulled out a book and began to leaf through it. He read odd pages, frowning, and stood there reading like that until three in the morning.

Leone now began to work with a publisher friend. There were only himself, the publisher, a storekeeper and a typist called Signorina Coppa. The publisher was a rosy-cheeked young man who blushed frequently. But when he wanted the typist he would shout 'Coppaaa!'

They tried to persuade Pavese to work with them, but he was unwilling and said 'I can't be bothered. I don't need a regular job. I don't have to keep anyone. All I need is a bowl of soup and some tobacco.' He had a part-time job in a school. He wasn't paid much but it was enough for him. He also made translations from English, including *Moby Dick*. He had done so, he said, purely for his own pleasure. He had been paid for it, certainly, but he would have done it for nothing. In fact he would have paid to be allowed to translate the book.

He wrote poetry. His poems had a long, slow, dragging rhythm, a kind of bitter melody. The world of his poetry was Turin, the Po, the hills, the fog, and the inns on the outskirts of the city.

He was finally persuaded to join the little publishing house. He became a punctilious and careful worker, grumbling at the other two, who arrived late in the morning and sometimes went off to lunch at three o'clock in the afternoon. He advocated a different time-table. He arrived early and went off on the dot of one, because his sister, with whom he lived, dished up the soup at one o'clock.

Leone and the publisher quarrelled from time to time, and did not speak to one another for a few days. Later they wrote each other long letters and were reconciled. Pavese 'did not care a damn about it'. Leone's great love was politics. This was his true vocation, but he was also passionately keen on poetry, philology and history.

He had come to Italy as a baby, and was as fluent in Italian as in Russian; he still always spoke Russian at home with his mother and sister. They seldom went out and never saw anyone, and he used to describe to them in the most minute detail everything he had done and every person he had met.

Before he went to prison he had enjoyed going to people's houses. Although he had a slight stammer he was a brilliant conversationalist; and although he was profoundly absorbed in serious thought and action, he was nevertheless quite happy to listen to the most trivial gossip. He was curious about people, and had an excellent memory, so he remembered the smallest details about them. But when he came out of prison he was not invited out in society any longer and people avoided him. He was now notorious in Turin as a dangerous conspirator. He was quite indifferent, and seemed to have entirely forgotten the parties of former days.

Leone and I got married, and we went to live in the apartment in Via Pallamaglio.

When my mother told my father that Leone wished to marry me he lost his temper, as he did with every marriage in the family. But this time he didn't say Leone was ugly; he merely said 'He does not have a proper job.' This was in fact perfectly true: his job was certainly insecure. He could be arrested and incarcerated once more: on any pretext he could be put into restricted residence. If, on the other hand, Fascism were to come to an end, he would become an

108

important politician, my mother said. Furthermore, although the little publishing house in which he worked was small and poor, it had great potential. 'They are even publishing Salvatorelli,' said my mother. Salvatorelli's name was endowed in my parents' eyes with magic powers. At the mention of it my father became gentle and kind.

So I married, and afterwards my father said, when he spoke of me to outsiders, 'my daughter Ginzburg'. He was always quick to stress this sort of change of status, and immediately started calling a newly-married woman by her husband's name. He had two assistants, one of whom was a man, called Olivo. The other, a woman, was called Porta. Then they got married but we continued to call them Olivo and Porta. My father would lose his temper and say, 'She is not called Porta any more; call her Olivo!'

GIUA'S son — that pale youth with smouldering eyes who had been so constantly with Mario in Paris — had died fighting in Spain. His father was in prison at Civitavecchia and in danger of losing his sight because of a cataract.

Signora Giua often came to see my mother. They had met at Paola Carrara's and had become good friends, though my mother continued to call her Signora Giua. She would say 'Tu, Signora Giua', because she had started like that and found it difficult to change. Signora Giua used to bring Lisetta, her little daughter, who was about seven years younger than myself. She looked exactly like her brother Renzo — tall, pale, thin and upright, with the same smouldering eyes, short hair, and a quiff. We went bicycling together, and she told me that she sometimes saw an old school friend of her brother Renzo at the Lycée d'Azeglio. He was very intelligent, she said, and he used to come to see her and bring books by Croce[29].

That was how I first heard of Balbo.[30] Lisetta told me that he was a count. She pointed him out to me one day on the Corso Re Umberto — a little man with a red nose. Balbo was to become my best friend many years later. But of course I did not know that then and I did not look with any interest at the little count who lent Lisetta Croce's books.

There was a girl whom I used to see sometimes going along the Corso Re Umberto whom I found very beautiful and quite odious. She had a face that seemed to be sculptured in bronze, a little aquiline nose which seemed to cut the air, eyes half closed, and a slow contemptuous walk. I asked Lisetta if she knew who the girl was.

'That is one of the d'Azeglio girls,' said Lisetta. 'She is a good mountaineer and thinks a lot of herself.'

'She is odious,' I said, 'odious and very beautiful.'

The odious girl lived on the ground floor in a street off the Corso. In the summer I sometimes saw her leaning out of the window, watching me through half-closed eyes, with a disdainful sneer and a mysteriously bored expression. Short brown hair framed her bronzed cheeks. I said to Lisetta: 'That face asks to be slapped!'

For many years when I was a long way from Turin I carried in my mind's eye the picture of this face 'asking to be slapped'. And when later on I was told that this same face was employed in the publishing house and worked with Pavese and the publisher, I was astounded that such a haughty disdainful girl should condescend to be with such simple people so close to me. Later I was still more astounded when I learned that she had been arrested with a group of conspirators.

In addition to Croce Lisetta also read Salgari's[31] novels. She was then about fourteen years old; an age at which one oscillates between childhood and maturity. I had read and forgotten Salgari's novels, and Lisetta told me stories when we sat down to rest in the country, laying our bicycles on the grass. Her dreams and her talk were a jumble of Indian rajahs, poisoned arrows, Fascists and the little Count Balbo who came to call on her on Sundays and lent her Croce. I listened to her half amused but without really paying attention. I myself had read nothing by Croce, except *La Letteratura della Nuova Italia*, or more precisely the summaries of novels and the quotations in that book. I had, though, written a letter to Croce when I was thirteen, and had sent him some of my poems, and he had replied very politely, pointing out in the kindest manner that my poems were not very good.

I took care not to let on to Lisetta that I had not read Croce, because I did not wish to disillusion her, since she thought so much of me, and I was comforted by the thought that even if I had not read Croce, Leone had read every one of his books from beginning to end.

It did not look as if Fascism would end soon — or indeed ever.

The Rosselli brothers had been killed at Bagnolo de l'Orne.

For years now Turin had been full of German Jews, refugees from Germany. My father had some as assistants in his laboratory. These people were stateless. We too might be stateless some day, compelled to wander from one country to another, from one police-station to another, without work or roots or family or home.

Some while after I was married Alberto asked me: 'Now that you are married, do you feel richer or poorer?'

'Richer,' I said.

'Me too,' he said, 'and yet when you come to think of it we are really much poorer.'

I was now buying our food, and I was astonished to find everything cost so little. I was astonished because I had always heard that prices were so high. Only sometimes I found myself without a penny before the end of the month, having spent all my money at the rate of thirty centesimi a time. I was glad now to be asked out to dinner. Even when invited by people whom I did not like, I was glad to be able, once in a while, to eat a free surprise meal, which I had not had to think about, or buy, or watch it cooking. I had a maid called Martina. I liked her very much but I could not help wondering 'Who knows if she does the cleaning properly? Or the dusting?' Totally inexperienced, I was unable to tell whether my house was well-kept or not. When I went to see Paola, or my mother, I would see clothes hanging up in the ironing-room to be brushed or cleaned with petrol to get stains out. I immediately started to ask myself 'Who knows if Martina ever brushes our clothes or gets the stains out.' There was a brush in our kitchen all right, and a bottle of petrol with a rag for a stopper, but that bottle was always full and I could not see that Martina ever used it.

I wanted sometimes to tell Martina to spring-clean the flat as I had seen done at home when Natalina, with a scarf round her head like a pirate, turned all the chairs upside down and whacked them with a carpet-beater. But I could never find the right moment to tell Martina what to do. I was shy and she was also very shy, and timid. We exchanged friendly smiles when we met in the passage, and I put off day after day suggesting a big spring-clean.

I did not in any case dare to give her any orders, though as a girl at home I used to give orders without compunction, and said what I wanted all the time. I remembered how on holidays in the mountains I used to have big buckets and jugs of hot water brought up to my room. There was no bathroom in the house so I washed in my room in a kind of hip-bath. My father was an advocate of cold water, but except for my mother none of us was in the habit of taking cold baths; in fact we children all hated cold water from our earliest years, purely out of contradiction. But now I was amazed that I had once been able to make Natalina heat the water on the stove, and climb the stairs with those large buckets. I would never dare to order Martina to bring me even a glass of water. When I got married I had suddenly discovered what work was. A kind of laziness came over me which sapped my will, and paralysed, so I thought, the people round me. As a result I imagined I was surrounded by complete inertia.

I made a point of ordering dishes for dinner that Martina could prepare quickly and which used the minimum of cooking pans. I also discovered about money. I don't mean I became stingy — like my mother I always had holes in my pockets — but I had identified the presence of money behind everyday things which take you who knows where on the track of thirty centesimi to unknown destinations, and this gave me a sense of strain and laziness and languor as well. I did not fail, however, to spend money at once when I had it in my hand, and immediately to regret having spent it.

I had three friends who were known in the family as 'the flixies'. In my mother's language this meant little girls with affectations and too many frills and frippery. These friends were not, I thought, either affected or over-dressed. My mother, however, called them flixies, harking back to the days of my childhood and to snooty little girls with frills who used to play with me in those days.

'Where is Natalia?' 'Oh, she is with the flixies' they always said in the family. These friends went back to my high school days; before I married I used to spend the day with them. They were poor and that may have been one of the main things that attracted me to them. I knew nothing about poverty but I liked the idea and would have liked to know about it. After I married I continued to see these three girls, but rather less frequently than before. Sometimes I did not go and see them for days. They reproached me for this although they knew it was inevitable. All the same, seeing them from time to time cheered me up and took me for a moment back to my adolescence which I could feel I was leaving behind.

For various reasons, these three friends lived in open opposition to society. In their eyes society meant an easy, well-ordered bourgeois life, based on regular time-tables, recreation and systematic pursuits arranged by the family. This was the life I led before I married and I enjoyed its many privileges. But I did not like it and aspired to get out of it, so with my friends I sought out the dreariest places in the city for our meetings; the most desolate public gardens, the most squalid milk-bars, the grubbiest cinemas, and the barest and emptiest cafés, and in the dingy gloom of these places, sitting on cold benches, we felt as though we were on a ship which had broken from its moorings and was drifting.

Two of the flixies were sisters who lived alone with their father who had once been very rich but had been ruined. He had a lot of business with lawyers over a lawsuit. He was constantly engaged in writing long petitions, and in travelling to and fro between Turin and Sassi, where he still owned a small property. The old man cooked elaborate Jewish dishes which his daughters did not like, and he lived in complete ignorance of what they did with themselves, which was anyway nothing out of the ordinary. They had constructed their own code of living in which paternal authority had no value and which consisted of only the occasional querulous remonstrance. Both girls were tall, flourishing, pretty brunettes. One was lazy and was generally to be found lying on her bed. The other was energetic and determined. The lazy one treated her father with good-humoured intolerance; the other one was uncompromisingly and contemptuously intolerant of him.

The lazy sister had almond-shaped Arab eyes, soft black curls, was rather less podgy and mad on pendants and ear-rings. And although she maintained that she hated being fat she did nothing to counteract it, and was thoroughly happy and serene about being podgy, and used to say of herself with a smile that revealed her large white projecting teeth, 'Nigra sum sed formosa'.[32] The other sister was thin and would have liked to be even thinner. She would anxiously examine her legs, which were as strong as pillars, in the looking-glass, for though she had made herself thin by sheer will-power, she had large hips and heavy, solid bones. If she had a date with a boy she was keen on, she ate nothing for lunch or only an apple. This was because she made her own dresses, and made them so tight that she was afraid they might split if she ate a whole meal. Nervously she devoted meticulous attention to those dresses, with a big frown and her mouth full of pins. She wanted them to be as simple and quiet as possible, as apart from her podginess she hated her sister for her tendency to dress in showy silk.

Every time their father went out he left on the kitchen table long notes of complaint, written in his pointed sloping hand, like a lawyer's: either about the servant 'who had received her fiancé by grace of one half melon gone as I found this evening'; or about the woman at Sassi who had let some 'darling little rabbits' die through neglect; or about a neighbour who had taken offence over a blanket lent at their request which had been returned with scorches; 'he had reproved her, and had not had words of protection for her'.

The girls often went to see some German Jewish refugees, and sometimes shared with them the mysterious dishes which their father had cooked and left in the kitchen in a big black frying-pan. At their house I used to meet these students, who lived from day to day, and did not know what they would be doing the following month, whether they would succeed in leaving for Palestine or would join some unknown cousins in America. For me the fascination of that house was unfailing and profound. It was always open to everybody. It had a narrow dark passage in which one tripped over the father's bicycle; there was a small sitting-room encumbered with elaborate shabby furniture, Jewish candelabra, and little apples from the property at Sassi, laid out on the worn carpets. Sometimes one met the old man on the stairs or in the passage. He was always absorbed in his legal business and official documents, or busy carrying hampers of apples and green peppers up and down the stairs. He used to talk to us in Piedmontese dialect about his lawsuit, stroking his grey unkempt beard and mopping his noble patriarchal brow under his hat. His daughters told him impatiently to go off to his own room.

There was a succession of ghostly and dim-witted women in this establishment. They were not, however, allowed to cook because the father wished to reign in the kitchen in solitary splendour, and as they were not allowed even to sweep the sitting-room because of the candelabra which they might break or the apples which they might steal, it was difficult to see what these women could do. In any case they were each dismissed after a few weeks, and another one, no less dim-witted and ghostly, joined the household.

The house was in Via Governolo. It was destroyed in the war, and on my return to Turin after the war I went to look for it. There was nothing but a heap of ruins in the old courtyard. Only the bannister remained of the gutted stairs up and down which the father used to go with his bicycle and the hampers. The old man had died some time before, during the war but before the German occupation. He fell ill and was admitted to the Jewish hospital, taking with him a chicken which he hoped they would allow him to cook. He died alone. One of his daughters had married and was in Africa, and the other, the determined one, was in Rome studying law at the university.

115

My third friend was Marisa. She lived in the Corso Re Umberto, but at the far end where it became a grassy space, the road ended and there was a tram terminus. Marisa was small and elegant, and never stopped smoking, and knitting pretty little hats which she wore at a very elegant angle on her curly red hair. She also made pullovers. 'I am making myself a pwetty pullover' — she could not say her 'r's. She had a great variety of 'pwetty pullovers' with turtle-neck collars which she wore under her camel-hair overcoat. In her childhood her parents had been very well off, and used to stay at health resorts and in luxury hotels, and while still almost a child she used to go dancing at seaside resorts. Later her family ran into financial difficulties. She looked back on that life — although so recent, by now ancient history — with a mixture of affection and irony, but without any bitterness or regret. She was by nature trusting, lazy and serene.

During the German occupation Marisa joined the partisans and displayed an extraordinary courage which one would never have suspected in the lazy, frail young girl she had always been. Later she became an official in the Communist Party and devoted her life to the Party. She only ever talked about Party matters, and was modest, unassuming and unselfish. She never married because no man ever lived up to the ideal she had clung to, a man she could not describe but whose qualities were in her imagination quite unmistakable.

These three friends were Jewish. The racial campaign had begun in Italy but they were unconsciously prepared for an uncertain future because of their contact with the Jewish refugees. Anyway they were quite carefree enough to accept the situation without the slightest sign of panicking. But apart from the energetic and determined one, all four of us worked haphazardly and rather half-heartedly.

As for my friends' old father in the Via Governolo, at the beginning of the racial campaign he received a form in which he was told to state 'distinctions and special services'. He answered: 'In 1911 I was a member of the *Rari Nantes*[33] club, and I dived into the Po in mid-winter. Once when building operations were being carried out in my house, the contractor Casella nominated me as foreman.'

My mother was not jealous of my three friends, as she always was of Paola's. She did not suffer or cry over my marriage as she had done when Paola was married. She had never treated me as an equal but had always been maternal and protective. Nor did she mind my leaving home, partly because, as she used to say, I never 'unwound'

116

with her. It was also to some extent because now she was getting old she was resigned to the gap which her children left when they went away. She had padded and protected her life so that she did not feel the shock of that separation.

IT SEEMED as though the only optimists left in the world were my mother and Adriano. Brooding uneasily in her little sitting-room Paola Carrara still invited Salvatorelli round in the evening, vainly expecting to hear words of hope. But Salvatorelli seemed to be full of gloom. Everyone was more and more dark and gloomy, and no one said anything hopeful: all were pervaded by a vague sense of fear.

Adriano however knew from 'one of his sources' that Fascism had a brief expectation of life. My mother cheered up when she heard this and clapped her hands. Yet at times a suspicion crept in that Adriano's famous source was a palmist. He was in the habit of consulting palmists, and knew one of these ladies in every city he visited. He said that some were very good and had accurately described his own past, and some even 'read minds'. Adriano considered thought-reading a fairly common ability. He would speak about something his father knew, and when one asked him how he knew it, he replied quite calmly: 'I can mind-read'. My mother always welcomed Adriano with great eagerness, partly because she was fond of him and also because she always expected him to have news which would bolster her optimism. Adriano in fact used to foretell for us all the most lofty and fortunate destinies. Leone, he said, would become a most important person in the government. 'How lovely,' said my mother, clasping her hands and behaving as though this had already happened. 'Will he be Prime Minister?' she asked. 'And what about Mario?' Adriano had more modest plans for Mario. He did not much like him and said he was too critical. He also considered that he had done badly to detach himself from the Rosselli brothers' group. Perhaps he still had an unconscious grudge against him for working in the factory so many years ago, and then immediately joining a conspiracy, getting arrested, and escaping. 'And Gino? And Alberto?' my mother went on to ask, and Adriano good-naturedly foretold their futures.

My mother did not believe in palmistry. However she played patience every morning, in her dressing-gown, while she drank her coffee in the dining-room. She would say, 'Let us see if Leone is to

118

become a great man in the government. Let us see if Alberto is to become a great doctor. Let us see if someone is going to give me a nice little house in the country.' Who would give her a nice little house was far from clear, certainly not my father, who was more anxious than ever about money; he appeared once more to have less than ever now that the racial campaign was under way. 'Let us see if Fascism is going to last,' said my mother, shuffling the cards and shaking her grey hair, which was always soaking wet in the morning, and pouring herself more coffee.

When the racial campaign started the Lopezes left for Argentina. All the Jews we knew were leaving Italy or preparing to go. Leone's brother Nicola had emigrated with his wife to America. He had an uncle there, Uncle Kahn, whom he had never actually seen, because he had left Russia as a boy. Leone and I also sometimes talked of going to 'Uncle Kahn in America'. However, they had taken away our passports. Leone had lost his Italian citizenship and was now stateless. 'If only we had a Nansen passport!' I would say. 'If only we had a Nansen passport!' This was a special passport granted to important stateless persons. Leone had once told me about it. To have a Nansen passport seemed the best thing in the world. However, at heart neither he nor I wished to leave Italy. At a time when it would probably still have been possible for him to leave, he had been offered work in Paris, with the group to which Rosselli had belonged. He had refused. Leone did not want to be an *émigré*, an exile.

All the same, we thought of the exiles in Paris as marvellous, miraculous beings, and it seemed extraordinary that one could meet them in the street there, touch them and shake hands with them. I had not seen Mario for years: I didn't know when I would see him again. He too was a member of that marvellous crowd: Garosci, Lussu,[34] Chiaromonte, Cafi. Apart from Chiaromonte, whom I had met at Paola's house at the seaside, I had never seen any of them. 'What is Garosci like?' I asked Leone. Paris was over there, not so far away, I used to think as I walked down the Corso Francia. I really thought of Paris as being just at the end of the Corso Francia, the other side of the mountains, behind that veil of blue mist. In reality we were separated from Paris by a vast chasm.

The men who were in prison seemed equally inaccessible and miraculous: Bauer and Rossi, Vinciguerra, Vittorio. They seemed to get farther and farther away, to sink deeper and deeper into the distance, like the dead. Was it possible that only recently Vittorio had been walking up and down the Corso Re Umberto with his jutting-out chin? Had we really once played the game of vegetable and mineral with him and Mario?

My father had now lost his chair in the university. He was invited to work in an Institute in Liège. He accepted, and my mother accompanied him to Belgium. She remained there for a few months; but she was very unhappy and wrote despairing letters. It was always raining in Liège — 'What a hole Liège is!' my mother said. 'What a hole Belgium is!' Mario wrote to her from Paris that Baudelaire could not stand Belgium either. My mother did not like Baudelaire very much: her poet was Paul Verlaine. Now she took a great liking to Baudelaire. My father, on the other hand, worked happily in Liège and had taken on a pupil, a young man called Chèvremont. 'Apart from Chèvremont and our landlady, I do not like the Belgians,' said my mother after her return to Italy.

She went back to her old way of life. She came to see me; she went to see Miranda and Paola Carrara; and she went to the cinema. My sister Paola had taken a flat in Paris and was spending the winter there.

'Now that Beppino is not here and I am by myself, I shall economize,' my mother was constantly saying, as she felt hard up. 'I shall eat little: some soup, some roast meat, and a piece of fruit.' She would recite this menu every day. I believe she liked saying 'a piece of fruit' because it gave her a sense of frugality. She used to buy apples in Turin called *carpandue*. She would say 'they are *carpandue*', just as she used to say a vest was 'from Neuberg's', or an overcoat was 'from Signor Belom's'. When my father happened to complain about the apples on the table and said they were awful, she exclaimed in amazement, 'Awful? But they are *carpandue!*'

'I wonder why I like spending money so much,' my mother would ask with a sigh. The fact was she could not achieve the régime of economy which she had prescribed for herself. In the morning, after her game of patience, she did the accounts with Natalina in the dining-room. They always squabbled over them; Natalina too liked spending because she had 'a hole in her pocket'. When Natalina cooked my mother said she made enough food for the parish poor.

'Yesterday, you cooked enough meat to feed the parish poor,' my mother would say, and Natalina would reply, 'If I cooks too little they shouts at me; if I do a bit too much they shouts at me; yesterday they says Tersilla were coming,' wagging her thick lips and gesticulating excitedly.

My mother said: 'Keep still. Don't wave your hands about. Your apron's dirty. Why don't you change? With all the aprons I have bought you, you have enough for the parish poor as well.'

'Oh, poor Lydia,' sighed my mother as she shuffled the cards and poured herself more coffee. 'The coffee you've made is dishwater. Couldn't you make it stronger?'

'It is the coffee machine that's no good. If they buys me another one, I have told 'em a hundred thousand times the holes are too big on this one; she goes through too fast. She ought to pass slowly, you know, coffee.'

'I wish I were a boy king!' my mother said. The two things that attracted her most in this world were power and childhood, and she liked them combined so that the first was tempered by the charm of the second.

'Look what an ugly thing I have become!' she said as she put on her hat in front of the mirror. She only put the hat on because she had recently bought it and it had cost a lot of money. She would take it off at the first corner in the street.

'They is a lot more than forty, they is more like sixty, because they is six years older than me,' said Natalina, brandishing her broom threateningly. She always talked in an excited voice and with a threatening expression.

'With that scarf on your head, you don't look like Louis XI; you look like Marat,' my mother said, and went out of the house.

She went to see Miranda. Miranda was wandering round the room, tired and pale. With her fair hair straggling her cheeks she looked as if she had been through a shipwreck.

'Wash your face in cold water, and come out for a walk,' my mother said. Cold water to her was a certain cure for laziness, depression and bad temper. She herself washed her face in cold water several times a day.

'I don't spend much — by ourselves, Natalina and I spend very little. Soup, a chop and a piece of fruit,' she recited.

'Don't spend much! A spendthrift like you!' said Miranda, and she went on, 'I have bought a chicken for today; I find chicken very convenient.' She pronounced 'chicken' with a curious intonation, a drawling nasal sing-song, which she adopted when she was contrasting her own household with ours and feeling a sense of superiority. 'It is one thing to be alone like you, and quite another to have Alberto who is never satisfied.'

MY FATHER stayed in Belgium for two years, and during that time many things happened.

To begin with my mother went to visit him now and again; but apart from the fact that Belgium depressed her, she was always fearful that international events might cut her off from Italy and from me. My mother had a protective feeling towards me which she did not have for her other children, possibly because I was her youngest child. When my children were born she extended to them the same protective feeling. In addition, she thought that I was always in danger because of Leone. He was arrested from time to time as part of security measures. When a political figure, or the King, came to Turin, he would be arrested and kept in prison for three or four days, and let out again immediately the person in question had left. Leone would come home with a growth of black beard and a bundle of dirty linen under his arm.

'The King's a devil of a nuisance!' said my mother. 'I wish he would stay at home a bit more.' Usually the King made her smile, and she had nothing against him. She liked his having very short bandy legs and a hot temper. But she was annoyed at Leone being arrested every time, 'just because of that silly man'. As for Queen Elena, she could not stand her. 'A beauty!' — her term of disparagement — 'a peasant woman! A stupid thing!'

My first two babies were born a year apart while my father was in Belgium. My mother left home with Natalina and came to stay with me.

'Here I am back in Via Pallamaglio,' she said. 'It doesn't seem to me so bad now. Perhaps that is in comparison with Belgium. Liège is worse than Via Pallamaglio.'

My two babies delighted her. 'I like them both, and should not know which to choose,' she said, as though she was expected to choose between them.

'He is the most beautiful today,' she said. 'Which one?' I asked. 'Which one? Mine!' she said, and I still could not understand which one she was referring to since she continually transferred her preference from one to the other. Then Natalina always said 'she' when referring to either of the babies — both boys. She would say, 'Got to be careful not to wake her up. She is all odd if you wake her up, you have to walk her up and down for two good hours because she's odd-like.'

As it was very tiring to have two small babies to look after, and Natalina was too distracted and excited to devote herself to them, my mother advised me to find a dry nurse. She herself wrote to some of the old nurses in Tuscany with whom she had kept in touch, and a nurse arrived just when the Germans had invaded Belgium. We were all very worried and not feeling inclined to cater for a nurse, with her demands for embroidered aprons and wide skirts. Nevertheless, although my mother was very anxious about my father, of whom we had no news, she managed to buy the aprons, and actually cheered up to see the big Tuscan nurse moving about the house in a wide rustling skirt. I felt very ill at ease, however, and missed old Martina, who had returned to her village in Liguria because she could not get on with Natalina. I was ill at ease because I was permanently afraid of losing this nurse. I was afraid that she would consider us, with our simple ways, beneath her. In any case that big nurse with her embroidered aprons and puffed sleeves reminded me of the precariousness of my own position. I was poor, and without my mother's assistance could not afford a nurse, and I thought of myself as Nancy in *I Divoratori*[35] when she watches her little daughter from the window being led along the road by their magnificent nurse, and knows that in fact all the family's money has been lost at the casino.

We were extremely alarmed by the invasion of Belgium, but we trusted that the German advance would be halted.

In the evenings we listened to the French radio in the hope of reassuring news. Our anxiety grew as the German advance progressed. Pavese used to come to us in the evening, and also Rognetta, a friend of ours whom we saw frequently at that time. Rognetta was a tall ruddy-faced young man who rolled his 'r's. He had an industrial job and travelled frequently between Turin and Romania. We, who led a cloistered sedentary life, admired the way he appeared to be always on the point of catching a train or of having just come off one. He was probably aware of our admiration, and played up his role as a big business man. On his travels he picked up news. Until the invasion of Belgium this was always optimistic.

Afterwards it was dyed in inky black pessimism. Rognetta said that Germany would soon invade not only France and Italy, of course, but the whole world, and there would not remain a square inch where one could survive. Before he left he used to ask me how my children were, and I would say they were well. Once my mother said to him, 'Who cares if they are well or not if Hitler is coming to massacre us all?'

Rognetta always had very good manners, and when he said goodbye he used to kiss my mother's hand. That evening as he kissed her hand he said that one could probably still go to Madagascar, though. 'Why ever Madagascar?' asked my mother, and Rognetta replied that he would explain another time but just now he had to catch a train. My mother had great faith in him and at that time, in her anxiety, lapped up every word that was said to her. So that evening and all the next day she said over and over again, 'Why ever should he say Madagascar?'

Rognetta never had time to explain about Madagascar. I didn't see him again for many years, and I don't believe that Leone ever saw him again. As we had been expecting for some days, Mussolini declared war on England. That same evening the nurse left, and with great relief I watched her broad back disappear at the bottom of the stairs, no longer in her nurse's outfit but dressed in black cotton. Pavese came to see us. We said goodbye with the feeling we would not see him again for a long while. But Pavese hated farewells and went away, as usual hardly extending two fingers of a reluctant hand.

That spring Pavese would arrive at our house eating cherries. He liked the first cherries, the small watery ones, which he said 'tasted of sky'. We used to see his tall figure from the window as he appeared at the end of the street, walking rapidly while he ate cherries and flicked the stones at the walls. The fall of France is linked for ever in my mind with his cherries, which he gave me to taste when he arrived, pulling them out of his pocket one by one with his surly, parsimonious hand.

We expected the war to overwhelm us and turn all our lives upside-down. On the contrary, many people remained unaffected, living as they had always done. Just when everyone was beginning to think they had got off very lightly, and that there would be no upheavals of any sort, no homes destroyed, no flights or persecutions, suddenly bombs and mines exploded everywhere; houses collapsed and the streets were full of ruins, and soldiers and refugees. There wasn't a single person left who could pretend that nothing was happening — shut his eyes, stop his ears, or hide his head under the pillows — not one. That was what the war was like in Italy.

Mario returned to Italy in 1945. He may have been upset and depressed. When my mother kissed him on his sarcastic-looking jaw, he held out his sunburnt forehead with its sly wrinkles, instead. He was now quite bald, with a wide skull shining like bronze, and he had a neat, worn jacket made of silk which looked like felt — the kind one sees on Chinese shop-keepers in films.

These days he frowned seriously when he approved of people or things that looked valid, or when he showed that he appreciated new novelists or poets. He would say of a novel, 'It is good.' 'It is not bad.' 'It is pretty good.' (He always spoke as though he were translating from French.) He had given up Herodotus and the other Greek classics; at least he did not talk about them any more. The new novels he valued were mostly French ones about the Resistance. He seemed to have become more cautious in his judgment, or at least more cautious about what he liked, and not prone to sudden enthusiasms as he used to be. He was not, however, more restrained about attacking or condemning things; his hates provoked the same old uninhibited violence.

He did not like Italy. Almost everything seemed to him ridiculous and silly, badly thought out and badly constructed. 'Schools in Italy are a pain. They are better in France — not perfect but better. Everyone knows there are too many priests here. Everything is in the hands of the priests.'

'There are so many priests!' he said every time he went out. 'You have so many priests in Italy. We in France can walk for miles without seeing a priest.'

My mother told him of something that had happened to a friend's little son, many years ago, before the war and before the racial campaign. This child was Jewish. His parents had sent him to a state school, but had requested the teacher to excuse him from religious instruction. One day this teacher was not in school and there was a substitute who had not been told. When the time for religious instruction came, she was astonished to see the little boy pick up his satchel and prepare to leave.

'Why are you going away?' she asked.

'I always go home when it is time for religious instruction.'

'And why?' he was asked.

'Because I do not love the Madonna.'

'You do not love the Madonna!' cried the mistress in horror, 'Do you hear, children? He does not love the Madonna!'

All the children joined in, 'You do not love the Madonna, you do not love the Madonna!' The parents were obliged to take their son away from the school.

Mario liked this story enormously. He couldn't get over it, and he asked if it was really true. 'I never heard such a thing,' he said, slapping his thigh, 'never heard such a thing.' My mother was pleased that he liked her story so much, but she became tired of hearing him repeat that teachers like that did not exist in France, and could not even be imagined. She was fed up with hearing him say, 'We in France . . .' and with hearing him attack the priests. 'A government of priests,' she said, 'is a lot better than Fascism.' 'It is the same thing,' he said. 'Don't you understand that it is the same thing? Exactly the same!'

During the war years when we had not seen him, Mario had got married. This news reached my parents a little while before the end of the war. He had married, so someone informed them, the daughter of the painter Amadeo Modigliani. For the first time at the news of one of us getting married, my father kept calm: this seemed very strange and inexplicable to us and to my mother. Possibly my father had been so fearful for Mario during the war years, imagining that he was either a prisoner in German hands or dead, that now the fact that he had merely got married seemed like an unimportant incident. My mother was very happy and indulged in speculations about this marriage and about Jeanne, whom she had never met, but who she had been told resembled a Modigliani painting, with a hair style like the women in those pictures. My father merely observed that Modigliani's pictures were horrors. 'Daubings! Dishwater!' was all he said, and he seemed to look on this marriage with vague approval.

When the war was over a letter arrived from Mario. In a few laconic lines it said that he had married for reasons connected with his residence in France, and he was already divorced. 'What a pity!'

said his mother. 'I am so sorry.' My father said nothing.

When they saw Mario again he seemed unwilling to talk about his marriage and divorce. He let it be understood that everything had been arranged in advance, both the marriage and the divorce, and he gave the impression he thought marriage and divorce were as simple and natural as could be. In any case, he seemed unwilling to talk about anything that had happened to him during those years. If there had been times of privation, terror, disappointment or humiliation, he did not speak of them. But sometimes when he was relaxing, his hands pressed between his knees in his old familiar way, and a disappointed twist to his mouth, a kind of gently bitter smile, his tough face would be furrowed with unhappiness.

'Aren't you going to go and see Sion Segre?' my father asked him. He had imagined that he would immediately go and see Segre, who had been with him when he escaped to Switzerland.

'No, I am not going,' said Mario. 'We would not know what to say to each other.'

He did not want to go and see his brothers and sisters either, although he had not seen them for years. As he had said of Sion Segre, 'We would not know what to say to each other now.'

However, he seemed pleased to see Alberto who had returned to Turin after the war. He did not despise him any more. 'He must be a good doctor,' he said, 'he is not bad, as a doctor he must be quite good.' Mario asked Alberto about Cafi's illness, describing his symptoms and telling him the opinions of the doctors who were treating him. Cafi was living in Bordeaux. He was by now bedridden, had lost all his strength and hardly spoke any more.

Little by little we pieced together how Mario had lived during those years, from laconic, impatient remarks which he flung at us from time to time, snorting and shrugging his shoulders as though irritated that we knew nothing about it. During the German advance he had been in Paris, having left the school in the country where he had been teaching; he had gone back to live in his garret with his cat. Day by day the Germans were advancing, and he told Cafi that they must leave Paris. Cafi had a bad foot and did not want to move. Just at that time Chiaromonte's wife died in hospital and he decided to go to America. He embarked at Marseilles on the last civilian ship to sail.

Mario finally persuaded Cafi to come away with him. They left

128

Paris on foot when the Germans were less than a mile away, and it was no longer possible to find transport. Cafi hobbled along leaning on Mario, and they moved exasperatingly slowly. From time to time Cafi sat down to rest on the edge of the road, and Mario readjusted his bandages. Then they went on again, Cafi dragging his painful foot in the dust, with a slipper on and a thick sock with red darning.

They ended up in a village near Bordeaux. Mario was interned in a camp for foreign refugees. On his release he joined the *Maquis*. At the end of the war he was in Marseilles and a member of the purge tribunal. Chiaromonte left America and returned to Paris. Mario, Cafi and he were friends still. Mario never even thought of returning to settle in Italy, and in fact he had applied for French citizenship. He was economic adviser now to a French industrialist and had come to Italy with him by car, and was taking him round to see factories and museums. It was the Frenchman who drove all the time since Mario still did not know how to drive. My father and mother worried as to whether this job was secure in any way, or whether it was purely temporary and precarious.

'I'm afraid he may end up doing nothing in particular,' my mother said. 'What a pity! He is so intelligent.'

'Who is this Frenchman?' asked my father. 'He seems a very doubtful character to me.'

Mario did not stay in Italy longer than a week. Then he left again with his Frenchman, and we did not see him again for a long time.

129

THE NEW publishing house of former days had become big and important. A large number of people worked in its new premises in the Corso Re Umberto, the old office having been destroyed in an air raid. Pavese now had a room to himself, and on the door was a notice saying 'Editorial Director'. Pavese sat at a desk, with his pipe, correcting proofs with lightning rapidity. When he had nothing to do he read *The Iliad* in Greek, chanting the lines aloud in a sing-song voice, or he would work on his novels, crossing things out with furious speed. He had become a famous writer.

In the next room was the Publisher, a handsome rosy-cheeked man with a long neck, slightly greying hair on his temples, swept back like pigeons' wings. He had several bells on his table, and telephones, and he no longer shouted 'Coppaaa!' In any case Signorina Coppa was no longer there, nor the old warehouseman. Nowadays when the Publisher wanted anyone he pressed a button and spoke on the intercom to the floor below where there were a lot of typists and warehousemen. From time to time the Publisher paced up and down the corridor, his hands behind his back and his head slightly on one side, and looked in at the rooms where his employees were and said something in a nasal tone. He was no longer shy, or rather his shyness only came back occasionally when he had to interview strangers, and then it seemed not so much shyness as a cold and silent air of mystery. Visitors were awed by his icy luminous blue gaze, which scrutinized them and sized them up from the other side of the glass-topped table. His shyness had thus become an important instrument in his work; it had become a force with which outsiders collided, like dazzled moths hitting a light. If they had arrived confidently, with stacks of projects and proposals, at the end of the interview they found themselves oddly disconcerted and at sea, and with an unpleasant suspicion that they might possibly be stupid and simple and had cooked up projects which had no proper basis, in the face of that cold scrutiny with which they were silently dissected and investigated.

Pavese seldom agreed to receive visitors. He would say, 'I have things to do. I don't want to see anyone. To hell with them. I don't give a damn.'

On the other hand, the new younger members of staff welcomed interviews with visitors: they might introduce new ideas.

Pavese would say, 'We don't need ideas in this place, we already have too many.'

The intercom would ring on his table, and the familiar nasal voice sounded in his ear: 'So and so is downstairs. Please will you see him. He may have interesting proposals.'

'What do we want with proposals? We are up to the eyes in them anyway. I don't care a damn for proposals. I don't want any ideas.'

'Then turn him over to Balbo,' said the voice.

Balbo would listen to anyone. He never refused a fresh contact. He was defenceless against proposals and ideas. They all appealed to him, aroused his interest, put him in a ferment. He would lay them before Pavese. In he came, a little man with a red nose, serious — how serious he always was when he had a new proposition to put forward, when he thought he had set eyes on a new aspect of humanity, amazed as he always was in the presence of some new human form which appeared on his horizon, always ready to discern intelligence everywhere, he looked with his icy blue eyes, that were both sharp and innocent, defenceless and penetrating. Balbo would talk and talk, while Pavese smoked his pipe, and twisted his hair round his fingers. Then he would say: 'I think it is a cretinous proposition. Beware of cretins!'

Balbo replied that it was, certainly, to some extent a cretinous proposal, but that taken as a whole it was not so stupid, there was a good nucleus that could be vital and fruitful. Balbo talked and talked — he was always talking, he was never silent. When he had finished talking to Pavese he went into the Publisher's room and spoke to him. The Publisher rocked back and forth in his armchair, darted his cold clear gaze at him from time to time, doodled geometrical patterns on a sheet of paper, his spent cigarette between his lips and his legs crossed.

Balbo never corrected proofs: 'I am not capable of correcting proofs. I am too slow. It is not my fault.'

He never read a book right through. He would read a few sentences here and there and then get up to go and talk to somebody. A mere trifle was enough to excite his interest, to set him bubbling, and his thoughts in motion, which then ran on and on. He would remain there until nine o'clock in the evening, talking to the desks, for he kept no fixed hours and never remembered to go for lunch.

When the desks were deserted and the office empty, he would look at the clock, jump up, slip his overcoat on, pull his green hat down on his forehead, and go off down the Corso Re Umberto, small, upright, his brief-case under his arm. He would stop, however, to look at the motor-cycles and motor-scooters in the parking places. He had an enormous interest in all sorts of machinery and a particularly soft spot for motor-cycles.

Pavese said, 'Why does he always have to talk while other people are working?'

The Publisher said, 'Leave him alone.'

The Publisher had a portrait of Leone on the wall in his room, with his head bent a little to one side, his spectacles halfway down his nose, a thick mane of black hair, deep dimples in his cheeks, and his feminine hands. During the German occupation Leone had died in the German wing of the Regina Coeli prison in Rome, one icy February.

I had never seen the three of them together again — Leone, the Publisher, and Pavese — after that spring when the Germans were invading France, except for one single occasion when Leone and I had come from the enforced residence where he had been sent immediately after Italy entered the war. We had a permit for just a few days; and we often had supper together — Pavese, the Publishers, my husband and I — and others who were beginning to be important in the publishing house, and still others who had come from Milan and Rome with suggestions and ideas. Balbo was not with us because at that time he was serving on the Albanian front.

Pavese hardly ever spoke of Leone. He did not like speaking of the absent or the dead. He said as much. He said, 'When one of us goes away or dies, I try not to think about it, because I do not like suffering.'

All the same, the loss of Leone did at times distress him. He had been his best friend. That loss may have been one of the things that tortured him. He was incapable of sparing himself pain and he went through the most bitter and cruel suffering every time he fell in love. Love overtook him like a bout of fever. It lasted a year or two years, and then he was cured but he seemed to be reeling with exhaustion, like someone who has just got up after a serious illness.

That spring, the last that Leone worked regularly in the publishing business, when the Germans were over-running France and everyone in Italy was expecting war, seemed to be farther and farther away. Even the war gradually faded into the distance. Since the central heating ceased to function on account of the war there had been brick stoves in the office. Then the hot water system was repaired, but the stoves remained there for a long time. Finally the Publisher had them taken away. Manuscripts lay in heaps all over the rooms because there were not enough shelves. Later Swedish bookcases with movable shelves were made, which went up to the ceiling. At the end of the corridor the wall was painted black, and prints and reproductions were fixed to it with drawing-pins. Later the drawing-pins were got rid of, and real pictures in glossy frames were hung there.

DURING the German invasion my father was in Belgium. He remained at Liège until the last moment, at work in the Institute. He could not believe that the Germans would advance so quickly, because he remembered the First World War when the Germans had been halted at the gates of Liège for a fortnight. Now, however, the Germans were on the point of entering the city, and he decided at last to close the Institute, already deserted, and to get away. He went to Ostend, walking part of the way among the crowds which thronged the roads and sometimes getting a lift. At Ostend he was picked up by a Red Cross ambulance in which there was someone who recognized him. He was made to put on an overall, and he went with the ambulance as far as Boulogne, where they were captured by the Germans. My father was brought before the Germans and gave his name. They did not trouble themselves about his name, which was unmistakably Jewish, but asked him what he was intending to do. He replied that he intended to return to Liège, and they took him back there.

He remained another year at Liège. He was alone there, since nobody was left at the Institute, not even his pupil and friend Chèvremont. He was then advised to return to Italy, and he did so, joining my mother in Turin.

They remained there until the house was damaged in air-raids. During raids he would never go down to the cellar. My mother always implored him to do so, saying that if he would not, she should not go down there either. 'Silly nonsense,' he would say on the stairs. 'If the building goes, the cellar goes too. You can't pretend the cellar is safe. It is nonsense.'

After this they were evacuated to Ivrea. When the armistice came my mother was in Florence. My father wrote telling her not to move. He remained in Ivrea, in the house of one of Piera's aunts who had been evacuated elsewhere. Then he was told to go into hiding because the Germans were looking for Jews and arresting them. He hid in the country in an empty house which some friends let him have. He had at last agreed to have a false identity card made for him, in the name of Giuseppe Lovisatto. When he went to call on acquaintances, and the maid who opened the door asked him whom she was to announce, he still gave his real name, saying, 'Levi — No, not that, I mean, Lovisatto.' Later they warned him that he had been recognized and he went to Florence.

My parents remained in Florence until the liberation of the North. There was very little to eat in Florence, and my mother used to say at the end of dinner as she gave an apple to each of my children, 'An apple for the little ones and the devil to peel them for the big ones!' She described how during the First World War every evening Signora Grassi used to take a walnut and cut it into four, saying 'One walnut, Lydia', giving a quarter to each of her children — Erika, Dina, Clara and Franz.

When Leone and I were living in the Abruzzi in restricted residence my mother enjoyed coming to see us. She also went to see Alberto, who was not very far away at Rocca di Mezzo. She compared one village with the other, and recited *La figlia di Jorio* which reminded her of those places.

As we had no room for her in the house, my mother used to sleep at the inn, the only one in the place. It consisted of a few rooms grouped round a kitchen, a pergola, a kitchen garden and a terrace. Behind it were the fields and low hills, bare and windswept. The owners, a mother and daughter, became our friends, and we used to spend our days in the kitchen or on the terrace, whether my mother was there or not. In that kitchen in the winter evenings or in the summer on the terrace, we discussed the entire village and the internees who like ourselves had come there owing to the war to become part of village life, sharing its ups and downs and problems. Like us my mother had learned the village nicknames of both the internees and the villagers. There was a large number of internees, of whom some were rich and others very poor. The rich ones ate better, and could buy flour and bread on the black market. But apart from their food, they lived the same life as the poor ones, sitting sometimes in the kitchen or on the terrace of the inn, or at other times in Ciancaglini's drapery shop.

There were the Amodajes, rich hosiery wholesalers from Belgrade, a shoemaker from Fiume, a priest from Zara, and a dentist; two brothers, German Jews, of whom one was a dancing master, and the other a philatelist; their names were Bernardo and Villi. Then there was a crazy old Dutch lady who was known in the village as 'Spindleshanks', because her legs were so thin; and many others.

Some years before the war 'Spindleshanks' had published some volumes of poetry in praise of Mussolini.

'I wrote verses in praise of Mussolini. What a mistake!' she said to my mother when she met her in the street, and she raised to the heavens her long hands in white gloves like a musketeer's, which had been a present to her from some society for Jewish refugees. All day long 'Spindleshanks' went up and down the street, walking along in a half-witted state and stopping to talk to people to whom she recounted her misfortunes, her gloved hands raised to the heavens. All the internees used to promenade up and down like this, taking the same walk a hundred times a day, because they were forbidden to go out into the country.

'Do you remember "Spindleshanks"? What happened to her?' my mother asked many years later.

When my mother came to visit us in the Abruzzi, she always brought a rubber tub with her, because no baths existed there and her constant anxiety was somehow to take a bath in the morning. She had brought a tub for us too, and made me wash the children several times a day. This was because in every letter he wrote my father urged me to wash them as much as possible, since we were in a primitive village, lacking any standards of hygiene. A servant we had at that time used to say contemptuously every time she saw us bathing the children: 'They are clean as gold. You are always washing 'em.'

This woman, a fat creature dressed in black and in her fifties, had a father and mother, both still alive, whom she called 'the old man' and 'the old woman'. Before leaving in the evening she wrapped up some paper bags of sugar and coffee, and put a bottle of wine under her arm: 'With your permission I am taking something for the old woman and a little wine for the old man because he likes wine.'

Alberto was transferred to a place farther north. This was considered a good thing: anyone moved to the north would in all probability be set free quite soon. From time to time we too put in applications to be transferred. But we would have been sorry to leave the Abruzzi, just as Miranda and Alberto regretted going, since they found their new place of residence at Canavese in Piedmont stupid. Anyhow our applications for a transfer fell on deaf ears.

My father occasionally came to see us. He found the village filthy:

it reminded him of India. 'It is like India,' he said. 'The filth in India cannot be imagined. The filth I saw in Calcutta, in Bombay!' He thoroughly enjoyed talking about India. He lit up with lively pleasure when he spoke of Calcutta.

When my daughter Alessandra was born my mother stayed a long time with us. She didn't feel like going away again. It was the summer of 1943 and it was hoped the war would end soon. It was a period of calm, and those were the last months that we spent together, Leone and I. In the end my mother departed, and I took her to Aquila. While we were waiting in the piazza for the bus, I had a presentiment of long separation. In fact I vaguely felt I was never to see her again.

July 25th came, the day of Mussolini's downfall, and Leone left restricted residence and went to Rome. I remained where I was. There was a field near us, which my mother called 'the dead horse field', because we had found a dead horse there one morning. I used to go there every day with the children. I missed Leone and my mother, and that field where I had been with them so often made me very depressed. My mind was full of gloomy presentiments. Along the dusty road between the hills scorched by the summer sun walked back and forth 'Spindleshanks' in her straw hat and with her ungainly walk. And the brothers Bernardo and Villi in long overcoats with half-belts, which had been given to them by some Jewish society and they put on in the height of summer because their clothes were worn to bits. With the exception of Leone the internees had remained there, because they did not know where to go.

Then came the brief exultation and delirious joy of the armistice; and then, two days later, the Germans. German lorries sped along the road; the hills and villages were full of soldiers: at the inn, on the terrace, under the pergola and in the kitchen. The village was petrified. I would take the children to the dead horse field, and when aircraft flew over we flung ourselves on the grass. I met the other internees constantly in the road, and we exchanged silent enquiring glances, wondering where to go, and what to do.

I received a letter from my mother. She too was frightened and didn't know how to help me. I realized then for the first time in my life that I was without any possible protection, that I had to cope by myself. I now saw that, bound up with my love for my mother, there had always been the confidence that she would protect and defend me in any misfortune. But now there remained only my love for her;

appealing for protection was no longer part of my love, in fact I saw that in future I might have to protect and look after her. For she was now very old, weak and defenceless.

I left the village on November 1st. I had a letter from Leone, brought by hand by someone from Rome, in which he told me to leave the village immediately, because it was impossible to remain concealed there, and the Germans would identify us and take us away. The other internees had now gone into hiding, scattered about the countryside, or in the nearest towns.

The local people came to my aid. They all put their heads together and helped me. The proprietress of the inn now had Germans established in her few rooms or seated round the fire in her kitchen, and she told them that I had been evacuated from Naples, was a relative of hers, and had lost my papers in the air-raids and needed to go to Rome. German lorries went to Rome every day. So one morning I climbed on to one of these lorries, and the local people came to kiss my children whom they had seen growing up, and we all said good-bye.

Once in Rome I breathed again and believed that this would be the beginning of a happy time for us. There was not much to justify such a belief. We found somewhere to live near Piazza Bologna. Leone was running a secret newspaper and was always out of the house. He was arrested twenty days after our arrival, and I never saw him again. I rejoined my mother in Florence. Misfortune always made her feel very cold and she wrapped herself in a shawl. We did not exchange many words about Leone's death. She had been very fond of him, but she did not like talking about the dead; her constant preoccupation was bathing the children, combing their hair and keeping them warm.

'Do you remember "Spindleshanks"? And Villi?' she asked. 'What do you think has happened to them?'

I learnt later that 'Spindleshanks' had died of pneumonia in a peasant's farmhouse. The Amodajes, Bernardo and Villi had gone into hiding in Aquila. Other internees were captured, handcuffed, and loaded on to a lorry. They disappeared down the road in a cloud of dust.

138

BY THE end of the war both my father and my mother seemed much older. Terror and disasters had aged my mother, suddenly, overnight. She always wore a shawl of mauve angora wool which she had bought at Parisini's. She wrapped herself up in it. She felt cold amid all the alarms and disasters, and became pale, with large dark rings under her eyes. The tragedies had beaten her down and weakened her; they made her walk slowly, taking the life out of her once triumphant step, and they carved two deep hollows in her cheeks.

My parents returned to Turin, to the house in Via Pallamaglio, which was now called Via Morgari. The varnish factory on the piazza had been burnt down in an air raid, and also the public baths. But the church had hardly been damaged and was still there, held up by iron tie-beams. 'What a pity,' said my mother. 'It might as well have collapsed, it is so ugly. But no, sir, it has remained standing!'

Our house was repaired and put in order. Boards were put in to replace some of the broken glass, and my father had stoves installed in the rooms since the central heating no longer functioned. My mother immediately sent for Tersilla, and once she had her in the ironing-room in front of the sewing-machine she drew a breath of relief and it seemed as though life might resume its old rhythm. She bought some flowered material to cover the armchairs which had been in the cellar, and were stained with mould in places. Lastly, Aunt Regina's portrait was hung up again above the sofa in the dining-room; once more she looked down on us with her round, clear eyes, her gloves, her double chin and her fan.

'An apple for the little ones and the devil to peel them for the big ones,' my mother invariably said at the end of dinner. But then she stopped saying that because once again there were apples for everybody.

'These apples are tasteless,' said my father.

'But Beppino, they are *carpandue!*'

My father told Chèvremont that he intended to donate to Liège

139

University his library, which had remained there. This was in gratitude for being received there during the racial campaign in Italy. He was in constant communication with Chèvremont. They wrote to each other and Chèvremont sent him his publications. My mother only thought of places in terms of the people she knew there. In the whole of Belgium no one but Chèvremont existed for her. When anything happened in Belgium — floods, or a change of government — she would say, 'I wonder what Chèvremont will say.'

Before Mario went there, the only person in France, for her, was someone called Monsieur Polikar whom she and my father had met at a conference. She always said, 'I wonder about Polikar . . .'

She knew someone in Spain called Di Castro. If she read about storms or high seas round Spain, she said, 'I wonder about Di Castro!'

In the course of one of his visits to Turin this man called Di Castro fell ill, and no one knew what was the matter with him. My father got him into a clinic and called in a posse of doctors. One said that it was possibly heart trouble. Di Castro had a high temperature, he was delirious and he recognized nobody. His wife came from Madrid, and was continually saying: '*Non è il corazon. È la cabezza!*' (It is not his heart, it is his head!)

Di Castro recovered and returned to Spain. Franco assumed power, the World War followed, and nothing more was heard of Di Castro. *Non è il corazon. È la cabezza!* my mother always said, recalling Spain and Senora Di Castro. The war swallowed up Monsieur Polikar as well. We did not even hear any more of Signora Grassi who used to live at Freiburg in Germany. My mother often remembered her, and would say: 'I wonder what dear Grassi is doing at this moment.' 'She may be dead,' she would say sometimes. 'What a terrible thought, that Grassi may be dead!'

Her geography was all confused after the war. She could no longer think calmly of Grassi or Polikar. They had had the power to transform distant countries into something homely, ordinary and cheerful, to make the whole world a town or street which she could go down in a moment in her thoughts, in the steps of those few familiar reassuring names.

After the war the world seemed vast, unknowable and boundless. However, my mother went back to living in the world as best she could, happily, for she had a happy nature. Her spirit could never grow old, and she never came to know old age, which means withdrawing into oneself, lamenting the break-up of the past. My mother looked upon the break-up of the past without tears, and did not mourn it. In any case, she did not like to wear mourning. She was at Palermo when her mother had died in Florence, unexpectedly and alone. She was deeply grieved, then she went out to buy mourning clothes. But instead of buying a black dress, as she meant to do, she bought a red one, and returned to Palermo with it in her suitcase. She said to Paola: 'What could I do? My mama could not bear black clothes, and she would be very happy to see me in this lovely red dress!'

> Alla Cia venne male a un piede
> Pus ne sgorgava a volte la sera,
> La Mutua la mandò a Vercelli.

> Cia had trouble with her foot
> Pus oozed from it often in the evening
> The Insurance sent her to Vercelli.

These three lines about Cia were part of a long poem about women in the rice-fields, the kind of verse that young poets wrote and submitted to the publishing house. After the war everyone believed themselves to be poets, and politicians. Everybody seemed to imagine that one could, or rather one should, write poetry about anything, after all those years in which it had seemed that the world was dumb and petrified, and reality had been seen, as it were, through a glass, in a state of crystalline, mute immobility. During the Fascist years novelists and poets had remained silent, and the few writers chose their words with the greatest care, from the scanty heritage of crumbs which were left over. During the Fascist régime poets found they could express only the arid circumscribed and mystical world of dreams. But now once again words were in circulation, and reality appeared again to be within arm's length. So the former fasters set to gathering these grapes with gusto. This vintage was universal since everyone thought of taking part, and the result was a confusion of language between poetry and politics which appeared mingled together. But then that reality suddenly turned out to be no less complex and secret, indecipherable and dark than that world of dreams. It was revealed to be the other side of the

141

glass, and the notion of having broken through that glass was seen to be a transitory illusion. As a result, many withdrew, discouraged and disheartened, and sank back again in a mood of bitter self-denial and deep silence. So the post-war period was gloomy and depressed after the first light-hearted post-war years. Many isolated themselves in the world of their dreams or in any work that would provide a living; work taken up haphazardly or in haste which seemed petty and colourless after so much excitement, though everyone forgot the brief illusory moment when they shared their neighbours' lives. For many years, of course, no one practised their own professions, but all thought that they could and should do a thousand things together, and it was some time before each man took up his own profession and accepted its burden and the daily fatigue and solitude, which is the sole means we have of contributing to the needs of others who are similarly lost and prisoners of solitude.

As for the verses about Cia who had trouble with her foot, they are moving, and did not seem beautiful then but clumsy, as indeed they are. At that time two styles of writing were fashionable: one was a simple enumeration of facts, in the wake of a grey damp reality in a bare lifeless landscape; the other was a violent delicious mingling of facts with tears, deep sighs and sobbing. In neither one nor other was there any selection of words, because in the first the words were absorbed into the greyness, and in the other they were lost amid the groans and sobs. The mistake common to both was the belief that everything could be transmuted into poetry and language, which meant that ultimately there was a revulsion from poetry and language, so strong that it carried with it true poetry and a true use of language. Everyone was reduced to silence, paralysed by ennui and nausea. We had to go back to choosing words, examining them in order to see whether they were true or false, to see if they had true roots or only the transitory roots of the common illusion. Writers were obliged to take their work more seriously. The time that followed was like a hangover, a time of nausea, lassitude and boredom, and everyone felt in one way or another that they had been cheated or betrayed. This was equally true of those who lived in the real world, and of those who possessed or thought they possessed the means of describing it. And so everyone went their own way again, alone and discontented.

Adriano came occasionally to the publishing house. He liked publishing and wanted to start a business of his own. But the kind of publishing which he had in mind was different from ours, because he did not intend to publish either poetry or novels. As a young man he had only cared for one novel: Israel Zangwill's *The Dreamers of the Ghetto*. None of the novels he had read later had made any impression on him. He had a great respect for novelists and poets, but he did not read them. The only subjects which interested him were town-planning, psychoanalysis, philosophy and religion.

Adriano was now a great and famous industrialist, but he still seemed to have something of the vagabond, just as he had as a young man, when he was doing his military service, and still had that dragging solitary tramp's walk. He was still shy, but he didn't know how to use his shyness as a forceful tool, in the way our Publisher used his. So he would conceal it in the presence of people he was meeting for the first time, whether they were political figures, or poor boys who came to ask for a job at the factory. He squared his shoulders, lifted his head and lit his eyes with a steady, pure, cold gaze.

I met him in the street in Rome one day during the German occupation. He was on foot, rambling around alone. He was dressed like everyone else but looked like a beggar in the crowd. At the same time he looked like a king, a king in exile.

Leone was arrested in a secret printing-works. We had a flat near Piazza Bologna, and I was there alone with the children; I waited for him. The hours passed and when there was no sign of him gradually I realized that he must have been arrested. That day passed, the night, and the following morning. Adriano came and told me to leave at once since Leone had been arrested; the police might arrive at any moment. He helped me to pack and dress the children, and we hurried away to some friends who had agreed to take me in.

I shall always remember, all my life, the great relief which I felt that morning on seeing before me the familiar figure I had known since I was a child, after those long hours of solitude and fear, during which I had thought about my own people so far away in the North, and wondered if I would ever see them again. And I shall always remember his back bending to gather up our belongings scattered about the rooms — the children's shoes for instance — and his good, humble and compassionate movements. As we left his face had the weary look it had had when he came to our house to take Turati away — that fearful, happy look he had when he was taking someone to safety.

When Adriano came to the publishing house he used to talk to Balbo, because Balbo was a philosopher, and he had a great liking for philosophers. For his part, Balbo was very much attracted by industrialists and engineers, factories and factory problems, machinery and engines. Balbo liked to show off to Pavese and myself, saying that we were intellectuals and he wasn't, and we didn't understand anything about factories or machinery. His passion led to admiring motorcycles parked on the road on his way home in the evening.

Adriano and Paola had divorced after the war: she was living in Florence in the hills at Fiesole, and he at Ivrea. He was still friends with Gino, however, and they saw each other constantly although Gino had left the factory at Ivrea after the war, and had gone to work in Milan. Gino was one of his very few friends, for Adriano was faithful to his friends and to the things he had discovered and known in his youth. He had remained faithful, for instance, in his inner self, to the novelist Israel Zangwill. This faithfulness was, however, only emotional and did not extend to the world of practical matters. He was always ready to set aside what he had done, and to look for new methods and techniques. He thought the things he was doing now would grow old before his eyes; in this way he was like the Publisher. He was also always prepared to scrap something which only yesterday he had decided on. He was always keyed up and restlessly questing for new ideas, a quest he put before everything. Nothing could stop him: neither consideration for the fortune which his old methods had brought him, nor the alarm and protests of all those around him, who had grown to like the old methods and could not understand why they should be cast aside.

By now I was working in the publishing house too. My father liked and approved of the publishing house, and my mother was distrustful and suspicious. My mother in fact considered that there was too great a left-wing influence in it. This was because after the war she had begun to be afraid of Communism, to which previously she had given no thought. Nor did she like Nenni's Socialism, which she found looked too much like Communism. She preferred

144

Saragat's party, although she did not wholly approve of them. She thought Saragat[36] had a face with no colour to it. 'Turati! Bissolati!' she would say. 'Kulischov! Now they were really good people. I don't like politics these days.'

She went to see Paola Carrara, who was still there in her little sitting-room, as dark as ever and full of artificial birds, postcards and dolls. Paola sat there brooding because she too was against Communists and feared they might gain control of Italy. Her sister and her brother-in-law were dead and she no longer had any reason for going to Geneva, and she did not read the *Zurnal de Zeneve* any more, and she could not wait for the end of Fascism or Mussolini's death since both had long since perished. So she was left with a violent antipathy to the Communists, regretting that the works of her brother-in-law, Guglielmo Ferrero, had not been republished in Italy, as after the end of Fascism they deserved to be. She no longer invited people to her sitting-room in the evening, because those who used to come, the old anti-Fascists, had gone to live in Rome where they had taken up political appointments. There remained my parents and a few others whom she would occasionally invite, but without her old zest. With the exception of my mother she found everyone too 'left-wing'. So she ended by falling asleep rather sulkily in her grey silk dress, with her hands gathered in the folds of her grey crochet shawl.

'You get so worked up about the Communists at Paola Carrara's,' said my father.

'Personally I don't like the Communists,' my mother replied. 'Paola Carrara has nothing to do with it. I don't like them. I love freedom. There is no freedom in Russia.'

My father admitted that there might not be much freedom in Russia. He was, however, attracted by the Left. His former assistant, Olivo, now professor at Modena, was on the Left. 'Olivo is left-wing too,' he said, and my mother commented, 'You see now you are worked up about Olivo.'

So my parents returned after the war to live in Via Pallamaglio, now called Via Morgari, with my children. I went to live with them. We no longer had Natalina. Immediately after the war she established herself in a garret with some furniture which my mother had given her and worked daily by the hour. 'I do not want to be a slave any longer,' she had said, 'I want freedom!'

145

'How stupid you are!' my mother said. 'How can you think I treat you as a slave? You are freer than I am.'

'I am a slave! I am a slave!' said Natalina in an excited threatening voice, shaking her broom; and my mother went out of the house saying: 'I am going out because I cannot stand the sight of you. You have really turned nasty.'

To work off her feelings she went to the greengrocer or the butcher. 'With me she is kept warm, she is never short of anything,' she said. 'Natalina really is a stupid woman.'

My mother went to Alberto's and Miranda's a short distance away on the Corso Valentino, and let off steam with them, too. 'Hasn't she got all the freedom she wants? I don't keep anyone as a slave,' she said.

Later she said, 'But what shall I do without Natalina myself?'

Natalina moved to her garret. However, she often came to see my mother who, to begin with, hoped that she would think better of it and return to her. Then she became resigned, and found another woman.

'Goodbye, Louis XI,' she used to say to Natalina as she was leaving to return to her garret, which according to her own account was 'splendid' and where she invited Tersilla and her husband to coffee in the evening. 'Goodbye to Louis XI, goodbye to Marat!'

Many of my parents' friends had died. Paola Carrara's husband had died even before the war. He was a tall thin man with a white toothbrush moustache. He always went about on a bicycle, in a little black cape that fluttered behind him. My mother always said he was so respectable. 'As respectable as Carrara,' she would say to give an example of the peak of rectitude, and even after his death she continued to say this. Adriano's parents had also died, in the months immediately following the armistice. First he and then she went, in a country place near Ivrea where they had been hiding. Lopez had died soon after returning from Argentina after the war. Terni too had died in Florence. My father still wrote to his wife Mary, though he had not seen her for a number of years. 'Have you written to Mary?' he would say to my mother. 'You must write to Mary. Remember to write to Mary!'

'Have you been to see Frances?' he said. 'Go and see Frances. Go and see Frances today.'

'Write to Mario. You be careful if you don't write to Mario today.'

146

Mario was no longer working with his Frenchman. He now had a job in broadcasting. He had become a naturalized Frenchman and had married again.

When he told us that he had married again, my father this time was angry, but only moderately. He and my mother went to Paris to meet the new wife. Mario was now living in a house by the Seine. The house was dark, and my father could not get a good look at Mario's wife. All he could see was that she was very small, and had a fringe falling over her eyes. When she was out of the room he asked Mario: 'Why have you married someone so much older than yourself?' In fact his wife was not even twenty and Mario himself was forty.

They had a baby girl. My father and mother returned to Paris when the baby was born. Mario was mad about her. He would walk her up and down the rooms: *'Elle pleure, il faut lui donner sa tétée!'* he would say excitedly to his wife, and my mother would say, 'He has become completely French.'

During this visit my father was infuriated one day to find Mario's first wife Jeanne in the house as well as his wife and baby. Although they had divorced, they were still friends.

My father didn't like the house by the Seine. It was dark, he said, and must be damp. As for Mario's wife, he thought she was too small. He kept on saying 'She is so small!' 'She is tiny,' said my mother, 'but she is charming. Her feet are rather too small: I don't like little feet!' My father wouldn't agree. His mother had had small feet. 'You are wrong. In a woman small feet are beautiful. My poor mama was always proud of having small feet.'

'They talk about eating too much,' he said. 'The house is too damp. Tell them to move to another.'

'You are mad, Beppino! They like living there so much.'

'Then there is the radio job. I'm afraid it may turn out to be nothing in particular,' said my mother.

'It is a pity,' my father said. 'With his intelligence he could have had a very fine career.'

Cafi had died at Bordeaux. Mario and Chiaromonte had collected together his scattered papers, written in pencil, and were trying to decipher them.

Chiaromonte in America had married again. He left Paris and came to settle with his wife in Italy.

Mario thought that he could not have done anything more stupid.

147

Still, they remained good friends and used to meet every summer at Bocca di Magra. They played chess together. Mario now had two children and worked for Unesco. My father wrote to Chiaromonte to ask what kind of work Mario was doing and whether it carried any guarantee of security.

'Perhaps this is not just nothing in particular, it may be a good job.' But despite having received reassuring information from Chiaromonte, my father shook his head disappointedly. He was obstinate and incapable of getting away from his first impression, and he clung to the idea that Mario had missed a brilliant and prosperous career.

And though he was still proud of having had in Mario a son who was a conspirator, and who had crossed the frontier many times with clandestine literature, and though he was still proud of his arrest and dramatic escape, nevertheless he still regretted the idea that he had caused the Olivetti family some risk and compromised the factory. So when some years later Adriano died and Mario sent a telegram from Paris: 'Tell me if suitable my presence funeral Adriano,' my father replied equally curtly: 'Unsuitable your presence funeral.'

My father was in any case always worried about one or other of his children. He would wake in the night and ponder over Gino. Gino had left Olivetti and had settled in Milan where he was a director and consultant to large companies. 'The last time he came here he seemed a bit gloomy,' my father said of Gino. 'I should not like him to have any worries. He has a lot of responsibility.'

Gino was the most faithful of us all to old family habits. He still went to the mountains on Sunday, both in winter and in summer. He still went sometimes with Franco Rasetti, who now lived in America but reappeared in Italy from time to time.

'Gino is such a good mountaineer,' my father said. 'He is very good. He is a very good skier too.'

'No,' said Gino, 'I am not at all good on skis. I do it the old way. But young people now, they are really good!'

'You are always modest,' my father said, and when Gino had gone away he repeated, 'Gino is so modest!'

'Mario is so intolerant,' he said every time Mario came from Paris. 'He never likes anyone. Chiaromonte is the only person he likes. I should not like him to be dismissed from Unesco. The political situation in France is not a bit stable. I am uneasy. It was so stupid of him to take French citizenship. Chiaromonte never did. Mario has been really stupid.'

My mother doted on Mario's children when he brought them to stay. 'Mario is so delightful with his children!' she said. 'He is so fond of them!'

'*Sa tétée! Il faut lui donner sa tétée,*' she said. 'They are completely French. The little girl is lovely, but she is quite wild. She is an arch-devil.'

'They don't know how to bring them up,' my father said. 'The children are much too spoilt.'

'And what is the point of having children if they are not spoilt?' my mother asked.

'He told me I am bourgeois,' my mother said when Mario left. 'He thinks I am bourgeois because I keep my cupboards tidy. They are very untidy about the house. Mario used to be so meticulous and so neat. He used to be just like Silvio. Now he has become quite different. But he is happy. Stupid fellow. He told me I was too right-wing. He treated me as if I were a Christian Democrat!'

'But it is true, you are right-wing,' my father said. 'You are afraid of Communism. You get worked up at Paola Carrara's.'

'Personally I don't like the Communists,' my mother said. 'I used to like the Socialists, once upon a time. Turati! Bissolati! Bissolati was so nice. I used to go to see him on Sundays with my father.

'This man Saragat is not so bad. It's a pity that he has a face with no colour to it,' said my mother; and my father bellowed: 'Don't talk such nonsense. You can't believe that Saragat is a Socialist. Saragat is right-wing. Real Socialism is Nenni's,[37] not Saragat's.'

'I don't like Nenni. Nenni might as well be a Communist. He always goes along with Togliatti.[38] I cannot stand that man Togliatti.'

'That is because you are right-wing.'

'I am neither right nor left-wing. I just want peace!' And she went out, her hat in her hand, and her hair, now white, floating in the wind, walking youthfully, rhythmically, exultantly again.

In the morning when she went out shopping she always stopped for a moment at Miranda's, and again in the afternoon on her way to the cinema.

'You are afraid of the Communists,' Miranda told her, 'because you are afraid they may take away your servant.'

149

'Well, if Stalin comes to take away my servant, I shall murder him . How could I manage without a servant, when I am no good at anything?'

Miranda was always sitting deep in an armchair, with a rug and a hot-water bottle, her fair hair tumbling down her cheeks and her childish sing-song voice.

Her parents had been caught by the Germans like so many luckless Jews who had not believed the stories of persecution. They were living at the time in Turin and it was cold there: so they went to Bordighera. Bordighera is a small place and everybody knew them there. Someone denounced them to the Germans, and they were taken away.

When Miranda heard that they were at Bordighera, she wrote and asked them for pity's sake to leave, as they were known to everyone there: the big towns were safer. But they had told her not to be silly. 'We are quiet people. Nobody does anything to quiet people.'

They wouldn't have anything to do with false names or forged identity cards. That seemed wrong to them.

They said, 'Who is going to touch us? We are quiet people.'

But the Germans did take them away, the little mother with heart trouble, so frank and cheerful, and the father tall, heavy and calm. Miranda heard that they were in prison in Milan. She and Alberto went there to try and reach them with letters, food and clothing. They did not make contact, and only later learned that all the Jews in San Vittore had been sent away to an unknown destination.

Using false names Miranda and Alberto went away with their child to Florence. They lived in two rooms near the Campo di Marte. The little boy caught typhoid and then came the air raids; they had to carry him, with a high temperature, to the shelter, wrapped in a blanket.

As soon as the war was over, they came back to live in Turin and Alberto reopened his surgery. There were always a lot of patients in the waiting-room, and in his white overall, a stethoscope dangling on his chest, Alberto would again slip away from time to time to the sitting-room, to warm himself by the radiator and to have a cup of coffee. He had grown fat and was nearly bald. There were still some feathery wisps of hair, soft, untidy and fair, on the crown of his head. Occasionally he decided to lose weight and began to diet. He tried out various free medical samples. But at night he got hungry and

150

went to the kitchen to find the leftovers from dinner in the refrigerator. They had a large refrigerator which Adriano had given them after Alberto had cured him once when he was ill. Miranda, who was always complaining, even complained about this present. 'It's too big,' she said. 'What am I going to put in it? I never buy more than a quarter of a pound of butter at a time.'

They constantly remembered the years when they had been interned in the Abruzzi, and looked back on them with regret. 'We were all right when we were interned at Rocca di Mezzo,' Alberto would say.

'Yes, it was really all right there,' said Miranda. 'I wasn't lazy. I used to go skiing with my little boy. I got up early in the morning and lit the stove; I never had a headache. But now I am always tired again.'

'You didn't get up as early as all that. Don't let us fantasize. You didn't light the stove: the woman came.'

'What woman? We didn't have a woman!'

The child, the former engine-driver, was now a growing boy. He used to play football with my children in the Valentino. He was big and fair, with a loud voice though slightly sing-song like his mother's. 'Mama,' he would say, 'can I go to the Valentino with my cousins?'

'Mind you don't hurt yourselves,' my mother would say, and Miranda would reply, 'Don't worry, they are as careful as snakes and as sure-footed as goats.'

'He's quite well-behaved,' Alberto and Miranda would say of their child. 'Who can have brought him up? It can't have been us. You can see he must have naturally good manners.'

'I may be going to the mountains on Sunday,' Alberto would say, rubbing his hands together. Like Gino, Alberto used to go to the mountains, but not the way his father had taught him. Gino went alone, or occasionally with his friend Rasetti at the most. He enjoyed the cold, the wind, the exercise and discomfort, sleeping little and badly, and eating little and in haste. Alberto, on the other hand, would go with a party of friends. He got up late and spent a long time in the hotel lounge chatting and smoking. He had a good hot lunch in the warm restaurant, a long rest in his slippers, and finally went out skiing. When he did ski, he too flung himself furiously into the exercise as he had learnt to do as a child, and as he could never do

151

things in small doses or judge his own strength correctly, he returned completely tired out, in a nervous state, with deep hollows round his eyes.

Miranda would have nothing to do with mountaineering. She hated the cold and the snow — except the snow in the old days at Rocca di Mezzo where she used to ski so well, she said, and which she was still nostalgic about.

'Alberto is so silly!' she said. 'He goes off to the mountains and always hopes he will enjoy himself, but he doesn't enjoy himself so very much, and he wears himself out. What fun is that? Anyway how can he expect to enjoy himself now? When we were young we enjoyed skiing or doing anything. Now we are not so young and we don't enjoy ourselves any more. It is one thing to do things when you are young, and quite another to do them now.'

'How depressing you are, Miranda!' said Alberto. 'You get me down — you clip my wings.'

Vittorio visited them occasionally in the evening when he was passing through Turin. He had been released from prison during the Badoglio government. He had then been one of the leaders of the Resistance in Piedmont. He belonged to the *Partito d'Azione*.[39] He had married Giua's daughter, Lisetta. When the Action Party broke up, he became a Socialist and was elected to the Chamber of Deputies. He lived in Rome.

Lisetta had not changed much from the days when she rode a bicycle and told me about Salgari's novels. She was as thin as ever, tall and pale, with hair falling over her glowing eyes. When she was fourteen she had dreamed of adventures. In the Resistance she had realized some of these dreams. She had been arrested in Milan and incarcerated in the Villa Trieste. Luisa Ferida[40] had interrogated her. Friends disguised as hospital orderlies had helped her to escape. Then she bleached her hair to avoid recognition. In between the escapes and disguises she had had a baby girl. For a time after the war was over her short chestnut hair still had blond streaks.

Lisetta's father had become a Deputy too, and travelled back and forth between Turin and Rome. Her mother, Signora Giua, still came to see my mother, but they quarrelled because my mother found her too left-wing. They also argued about the boundaries of Asia, and Signora Giua brought the de Agostini atlas in order to prove with documentary evidence that my mother was wrong. Signora Giua

152

looked after Lisetta's baby, because being still very young Lisetta did not yet feel like mothering her own daughter, who had been born almost without her having time to realize, since she had gone so suddenly from girlish dreams to adult life without a moment to stop and think.

Lisetta was a Communist and saw everywhere, and in everybody, remains of the *Partito d'Azione*, the PDA as she called it. She saw its shadow lurking in every corner. She told Alberto and Miranda: 'You are PDAs. You have an incurable PDA mentality.'

Her husband, Vittorio, watched her as one watches a kitten playing with a ball of string, and laughed at her, shaking his big shoulders and jerking his jutting chin.

'You can't live any more in Turin. What a boring city!' Lisetta said. 'Such a PDA city. I could not live there any more.'

'You are quite right,' Alberto said. 'We are bored to death here. Always the same faces.'

'Lisetta is so silly,' said Miranda. 'As if there were anywhere one can have fun. One can't have fun any more.'

'Let's go and eat snails,' said Alberto, rubbing his hands. They crossed the Piazza Carlo Felice: the colonnades were feebly lit and almost deserted at ten o'clock in the evening. They went to a small restaurant which was almost empty. There were no snails so Alberto ordered spaghetti. 'Aren't you on a diet?' asked Miranda, and he replied: 'Be quiet: you clip my wings.'

'Alberto is so tiresome,' Miranda complained to my mother in the morning. 'He is always restless, he always wants to do something, to eat something, to drink something, or to go somewhere. He is always looking for fun.'

'He is like me,' my mother said. 'I should like some fun too. I should like to go away on a nice long journey.'

'No, really!' said Miranda. 'But it is so nice at home. Perhaps I'll go to Elena's at San Remo for Christmas. But I don't know whether to go or not. After all what would I do there? I might as well stay here!'

On her return she reported to my mother: 'Do you know, I gambled in the San Remo casino? I lost. That fool Alberto lost too. We lost ten thousand lire.'

'Miranda and Alberto gambled at the casino in San Remo,' my mother told my father. 'They lost ten thousand lire.'

'Ten thousand lire!' bellowed my father. 'You see what fools they are! Tell them not to gamble ever again. Tell them that I absolutely forbid it!'

He wrote to Gino: 'That fool Alberto lost a large sum of money at the casino in San Remo.'

After the war my father's ideas about money had become more vague and confused than ever. On one occasion (during the war) he had asked Alberto to buy him ten tins of condensed milk. Alberto managed to get them on the black market, for more than one hundred lire each. My father asked how much he owed him, and Alberto said, 'Nothing, it doesn't matter.' My father then took out forty lire and said, 'Keep the change.'

'My Incet shares have gone down a lot, you know,' Miranda told my mother. 'I may sell them.' She smiled happily with that shrewd clever look she always had when she talked about making or losing money.

'You know Miranda is selling her Incet shares,' my mother reported, 'and she says that we would do well to sell our Property ones.'

'What do you think that silly woman Miranda knows?' my father shouted.

However, he thought it over and asked Gino: 'Do you think I should sell my Property shares? Miranda says so. You know, she understands the Stock Exchange. She has a lot of flair for it. Her poor father was a stockbroker.'

Gino said, 'I know absolutely nothing about the Stock Exchange.'

'Ah, that is true, you know absolutely nothing. In this family we have very little business acumen.'

'The only thing we are any good at is spending money,' my mother remarked.

'You certainly are,' said my father. 'I wouldn't say that I spend too much. I have had the suit I am wearing for seven years.'

'Yes, indeed, one can see that, Beppino. It is all worn, quite threadbare. You must get yourself a new one.'

'I wouldn't dream of it. What a thought! This one is still very good. How dare you tell me to get a new one!'

'Gino,' he said, 'isn't a spendthrift, either; he is very careful. But Paola does spend too much. You lot have holes in your pockets — except Gino. You are all megalomaniacs. Gino is very generous to

154

others, but doesn't bother much about himself. He is the best of the lot, is Gino.'

Paola occasionally drove up from Florence alone. 'You came alone? By car?' my father said. 'You shouldn't. It's dangerous. What would you do if you had a puncture? You should come with Roberto. Roberto knows a great deal about cars; he was mad about them when he was little. I remember that he talked about nothing else. Well, tell me about Roberto.'

Roberto was now grown up, and at university. 'I like Roberto very much,' he said. 'He is so sweet-natured. But he is rather too keen on the ladies. Mind he doesn't get married. Don't let him get it into his head to go and marry.'

Roberto had a motor-boat, and used to go cruising in the summer with his friend Pier Mario. On one occasion the engine broke down, the sea was very rough, and they had a narrow escape.

'Don't let him go out alone with Pier Mario in that motor-boat, it is dangerous,' my father said to Paola. 'You must assert yourself. You have no authority.'

'Paola does not know how to bring up her children,' my father said to my mother in the night. 'She has spoilt them too much. They do whatever they like. They spend too much. They are megalomaniacs.'

'Tersilla's here!' said Paola, coming into the ironing-room. 'How lovely to see Tersilla!' Tersilla stood up and smiled, showing her gums. She asked after Paola's children, and Lydia, Anna and Roberto.

Tersilla made trousers for my children. My mother's constant fear was that they might be short of trousers, or they would be 'out at the seat' she said. Because of this fear that they might be 'out at the seat' she was always having five or six pairs made at a time. She and I argued over these trousers.

'There is no point in having so many pairs made,' I would say, and she would reply, 'I know you support the Soviets. You are all for the austere life. I want to see the children properly dressed. I don't want them to be "out at the seat".'

When Paola was staying with us, she and my mother walked arm-in-arm along the arcades, chatting and looking at the shop windows. She could let herself go with Paola. She would tell Paola what she thought of me. 'She never unwinds,' she would say of me. 'She doesn't talk. She is too much of a Communist. She's a real Red. Fortunately I have my little ones.' By that she meant my children. 'They are such darlings. I am so fond of them. I like all three of them and shouldn't know which to choose. Fortunately I have the little ones, and so I'm not bored. Natalia would let them go "out at the seat"! But I don't: I keep them tidy. I get Tersilla to come.'

Belom, the old tailor, had died some time ago. Now my mother had her clothes made in a shop in the arcades called Maria Cristina. For jerseys and blouses she went to Parisini.

'It is from Parisini's,' my mother would say, showing Paola a blouse she had bought, in the same voice that she would say of the apples on the table, 'They are *carpandue!*'

'Come along,' she said to Paola, 'let us go to Maria Cristina's. I want to have a nice coat and skirt made.'

'Don't have a coat and skirt,' said Paola. 'You've got so many. Don't dress so Swiss. Have a nice smart black coat made, something impressive, that you can wear in the evening when you go to Frances'.'

My mother ordered a black coat. Then she found it fitted badly on the shoulders, and had it altered at home by Tersilla. But she never wore it anyway. 'It is too *grande dame*' she said. 'I might give it to Natalina.'

As soon as Paola left she ordered a coat and skirt. She appeared in it one morning at Miranda's.

'But why,' said Miranda, 'have you had another coat and skirt made?'

'Many clothes, great honour,' my mother said.

Paola had her own friends in Turin and sometimes arranged to meet them. My mother was always a bit jealous.

'How come you are not with Paola?' Miranda would ask, and my mother would answer, 'She has gone out with Ilda today. I do not like Ilda one little bit, she is not so very pretty, and she is too tall. I don't like women to be too tall, and she talks too much about Palestine.'

By this time Ilda had left Palestine, but she still continued to talk about it. Her brother Sion Segre had a chemical company. He and Alberto were still good friends. Alberto would say to Paola: 'Shall we go and eat snails this evening with Ilda and Sion?'

'I don't like snails,' my mother said, and she stayed at home to watch television. My father despised television. He said that it was all nonsense. All the same he approved of my mother watching it because it was a present from Gino; in fact if she did not turn it on in the evening but sat in a chair reading a book, he would say: 'Why haven't you turned on the television? Turn it on, otherwise there's no point in having it. Gino gave it to you and you don't look at it. You have made him waste his money on you; you might at least look at it.'

In the evening my father read in his study and my mother watched the television with the servant.

After Natalina my mother always had a servant from the Veneto; she got them from a place called Motta di Livenza.

One night one of these servants coughed blood; we were all very alarmed. An urgent call was made to Alberto who said that she must be x-rayed on the following day. The woman was in despair and wept. Alberto said he didn't think it was a haemorrhage from the lungs: he thought she had a scratch in her throat. The x-ray showed nothing. She did in fact have a scratch in her throat. The woman, however, wept and was in despair. My father said: 'These proletarians are always so frightened of death.'

Every time that Paola went away again my mother embraced her tearfully. 'I am so sorry that you are going away, just when I have got used to having you here.'

'Come and stay with me for a while in Florence,' Paola said.

'I can't,' said my mother. 'Papa won't let me and then Natalia goes to the office, and I have to look after my babies.'

When Paola heard her speak of 'my babies' she was a bit annoyed, because she was rather jealous of them. 'They are not your babies, they are your grandchildren. My children are your grandchildren too. Come and stay for a while with my children.'

Sometimes my mother did go. 'You will see Mary as well,' my father would say. 'Mind you go at once and see Mary.'

'I shall definitely go,' my mother said. 'I really want to see Mary. I like Mary.'

'Mary is so nice,' she said on her return. 'And she is so respectable. I have never seen anyone as respectable as Mary. I enjoyed myself in Florence. I like Florence; and Paola has that beautiful house.'

'I cannot stand Florence; I cannot stand Tuscany,' said my father. During the war when oil was not to be had, Paola had sent him some oil — she had olives on the land surrounding her house at Fiesole —

and my father was angry: 'I don't want oil! I can't stand oil! I can't stand Tuscany! I don't want these acts of kindness!'

'Paola didn't make an ass of herself with you, did she?' he asked my mother. 'No. Poor Paola! She sent me up breakfast in bed. I had a good breakfast in bed like that, in the warm. It was lovely.'

'So much the better. But Paola is an ass at times.'

'And who is to prevent you having breakfast in bed here?' Miranda asked her.

'Here? No! Here I get up and immediately have a cold shower. Then I have my games of patience, well wrapped up, well covered up, and so I get warm.'

She played patience in the dining-room. In would come my little girl, Alessandra, surly and angry because she did not like getting up or going to school, and my mother would cry, 'Here's Maria storm cloud!'

'Let us see if I shall soon go on a nice journey. Let us see if someone will give me a nice little house in the country. Let us see if Gino will become famous. Let us see if they are going to give Mario a more important job instead of that one with Unesco.'

'Rubbish,' said my father as he went past. 'Still your never-ending rubbish.'

He put on his raincoat to go to the laboratory. He no longer left before dawn. Now he went at eight o'clock. At the front door he shrugged his shoulders and said: 'Who do you think is going to give you a little house? You are nothing but a silly woman!'

I SPENT all my evenings at Balbo's. Sometimes I found Lisetta there, but not Vittorio. He came only rarely to Turin and when he did come he preferred to spend the evening with his old friend Alberto.

Lisetta and Balbo's wife Lola were friends. Lola was the odious and very beautiful girl whom I used to see at one time at the window or striding so disdainfully along the Corso Re Umberto. They had got to know each other during the years when I was interned.

When Lola had stopped being odious, I don't know. When she and I became friends, she explained to me that she had in the old days known very well that she was odious, and in fact she tried to appear as odious as possible. She was especially cramped by shyness, insecurity and boredom. To this day I look back with amazement on that old odiously haughty image, so odious that I felt a worm under her gaze, and I came simultaneously to hate both her and myself. I look back and compare the girl I knew then with my friend as she now is — the closest in the world.

While I was interned, Lola had worked briefly as a secretary in the publishing house. She was, however, a bad secretary and very forgetful. Then the Fascists arrested her and she was put in prison for two months. During the occupation she had married Balbo. She was still very beautiful, but she no longer wore her hair in page-boy style, like a steel helmet. Now it was untidy, and tumbled down her cheeks. It was Indian hair — not an Indian woman's but like a man's. The old hard, immobile profile, naked and beaten by bad weather, by sun and rain, had been transformed into an anxious frowning face. And yet at times, for a moment, there would be a glimpse of the old contemptuous profile, the old dawdling, disdainful walk.

Every time she was mentioned my father would immediately say: 'That Lola Balbo is very beautiful. Oh, she is very beautiful.' And he said: 'I know that the Balbos are very good mountaineers. I know they are friends of Mottura.'

Mottura was a biologist whom my father thought highly of. The Balbos' friendship with Mottura reassured him about my evenings there. Every time I went out in the evening, he said to my mother:

'Where is she going? Is she going to the Balbos? They are great friends of the Motturas. How come that they are such friends with Mottura? How come they know one another?' (My father was always anxious to know why one person was friends with another.) 'How does he know him? How did they meet?' he would ask restlessly. 'Ah, I dare say in the mountains. They must have met in the mountains.' Having thus settled the origin of a connection between two people, he calmed down, and if he thought well of one of them he was ready to acknowledge the other with kindly approval.

'Does Lisetta go to the Balbos too? How does Lisetta know them?'

The Balbos lived in the Corso Re Umberto and had a flat on the ground floor, the door of which was always open. People continually went in and out. Friends of Balbo who came with him to the publishing house, or followed him to the Café Platti where he used to go for his *cappucino,* came home with him and talked far into the night. If he was not at home when they came, they sat in the sitting-room just the same, and talked to each other, walked along the passages, and perched on the edge of his study table, since they had learnt from him not to have fixed hours, not to think of going to supper, but to argue interminably.

Lola was utterly fed up with having so many people in the house. However, she went on with what she had to do. She looked after her little boy with a mixture of nervousness and distaste. Like Lisetta she was not very good at being a mother, having passed from the mists of adolescence straight to the harshness of adult life, violently and without transition. She liked sometimes to leave the child with her mother or her mother-in-law, to dress up smartly, putting on her pearls and other jewellery, and then as in the old days to go out along the Corso Re Umberto, walking with slow steps and her eyes half-closed, and cutting the air with her aquiline profile. When on her return she found people still in the house just as she had left them, deep in conversation, seated on the settee in the hall, or perched on the tables, she gave a long throaty cry of exasperation, which nobody took any notice of.

When her husband was away she used to call him sweet names, and complain about his momentary absence with a long throaty cry, but affectionately, like a dove calling for her mate. But as soon as she saw him again she lost no time in scolding him, either because he was always late for lunch, or had gone out and left her without any

160

money for the housekeeping, or because she was annoyed by the front door being always left open and people coming in and out. And so they started quarrelling, he armed with clever quibbles and she with nothing but her fury. The rights and wrongs of the one and the other got inextricably tangled. In any case they were never alone, even when they were quarrelling. She would even shout insults at the friends who happened to be present, and yell at them to go away. But they never dreamed of stirring and waited with quiet amusement for the squall to pass.

Balbo always had the same things for lunch: risotto with butter, a steak, a potato, and an apple. That is what he had to eat because he had picked up an internal infection during the war. 'Have you got my steak?' he would ask fretfully as he sat down to a meal, and as soon as he was reassured on this point he began eating, continuing absentmindedly at the same time to talk to his friends, who were always present at meals, and to quarrel with his wife, arguing all the time with clever quibbles.

'He is so boring,' Lola would say, turning to his friends. 'I find him so boring. Yes, there *is* steak. These everlasting steaks are such a bore. If only he would eat fried eggs just once!' And she recalled Resistance days in Rome when they were in hiding and without a lira, and she had to run all over the city to find butter, steak and rice for him on the black market. Balbo explained that he could not eat fried eggs as they were bad for him; and he went on solemnly eating, quite indifferent to the sort of steak he had before him provided that it was unquestionably grilled and not fried.

'I don't like these friends of yours,' Lola complained. 'They have no private life. They have no wives or children, or if they have, they don't trouble themselves about them. They are always here.'

On Saturdays and Sundays the house was deserted. Lola left the child with her mother-in-law and she and her husband went skiing.

'He was such a darling yesterday,' Lola would say of her husband on Monday to the friends who had reassembled once more. 'He was such a darling; you should have seen him. He can ski like a maestro. He is like a ballet dancer. He wasn't boring at all. We had such fun. And now, you see, he is a bore again.'

She and her husband occasionally went dancing at night clubs far into the night. 'We had such fun,' Lola would say. 'He waltzes so well; he dances so lightly.' And as she hung up her dress in the wardrobe she gave for her husband, who was at that moment at the office, that throaty tender call like a dove's.

Balbo sometimes said to his wife: 'Buy yourself a new evening dress. I'd like that.' So in order to please him she would buy a new dress, and then she would be displeased with it, and find it was absurd and would never wear it. 'That stupid man!' she said. 'To please him I have had to go and buy a dress that is completely pointless!'

Lola had not worked since that brief period as a secretary in the publishing house. She and her husband agreed she had been a very bad secretary. They were equally agreed that there must somewhere be some work she could do: the thing was to find it. Balbo asked me too to find, in the immense variety of work to be done in the world, a job which Lola could do well.

Lola was always recalling nostalgically the time she spent in prison. In jug she had felt very at ease herself at last, at peace in her mind, and free from complexes and inhibitions. She had made friends with some Yugoslav girls who were inside for political reasons, and with some of the ordinary prisoners. She found the right way to talk to them and win their confidence. The women prisoners clung to her for help and advice. Conversations between Balbo and his wife on the question of a job for her always ended up 'in jug', and both came to the conclusion that they must look for a job where she could feel as at home as when she was in jug, free of inhibitions and completely on top of herself. Work of this kind, however, didn't seem easy to find. Later she fell ill and had to spend a short time in hospital. In hospital she regained to some extent her power of leadership, which evidently revived in moments of tension, danger and emergency.

Lisetta found a job in Rome with the Italy–USSR Association. With Lola and myself she had begun to learn Russian immediately after the war, and she had mastered it, while we had given up along the way. Lisetta went to the office every day; she also managed to run the house, and now looked after her children too. But she pretended that she was not looking after them, that although they were still quite small, they were quite independent. She still came to Turin in the holidays, and brought the children with her. When we asked her where they were, she would look vague and absentminded, and say she could not remember where she had left them. She liked to give the

162

impression that she had left them to play by themselves in the street. The truth was that they were in the public gardens with their grandmother and the nurse, who kept an eye on them; as soon as it was dusk she herself went with scarves and caps to fetch them. Without realizing it, and certainly without admitting it to herself or anyone else, she had become a tender, conscientious and anxious mother.

She also always pretended to be quarrelling with her husband about politics. In fact she was as gentle as a lamb with him, and quite incapable of holding opinions different from his. In any case there was no real difference between their political views. The *Partito d'Azione*, the PDA, was by now forgotten and no trace remained anywhere. But Lisetta always said that she could see its ghost creeping everywhere, and particularly on the walls of her own house. As soon as her children became capable of reasoning she argued with them too, especially with her eldest girl, who was self-important and sarcastic, and answered back smartly. So mother and daughter argued at length — about plates of meat, rich and poor, Left and Right wings, Stalin, priests, and Jesus.

'Don't play the countess like that!' Lisetta would say to Lola when she saw her putting on her jewellery and making up in front of her looking-glass. She would end up herself putting on a dash of black round the eyes — the merest suspicion. Then they would go out along the Corso Re Umberto and the main streets, Lisetta in a black overcoat with large buttons, a brooch pinned to the lapel, and her pointed aquiline nose cutting the air, and her old swinging disdainful walk.

They went to the publishing house and found Balbo in the corridor talking to a priest, to Mottura, or to some of the friends who had followed him from his house. 'He spends too much time with priests,' Lisetta said. 'There are too many of them.' She didn't say 'he has a PDA mentality' about him. He was one of the few people about whom she did not say that, and Balbo at times accused her of herself being a bit PDA, possibly the last PDA left. She retaliated by accusing him of being too Catholic. She was ready nevertheless to forgive him that, as she would never have forgiven anyone else, because she could remember how when she was a child she had been fascinated by what Balbo said when he brought her books by Croce on Sundays.

'A count! At heart he is a count. They are a count and countess at heart,' she said of Balbo and his wife when she was far away from them in Rome. She saw other friends in Rome whom she liked much less, with whom she had no differences, but no close ties of memory either, and with whom in fact she got rather bored. But she did not admit that to herself. The fact that Balbo was from a noble family and a Catholic seemed to invalidate the arguments they had when they were together. But every time she came back to Turin, the Balbos' house attracted her overwhelmingly, but she still could not tell herself the truth and say, 'They are my friends, and I am fond of them, and it doesn't matter a scrap to me whether their opinions are true or false, and I couldn't care less that he likes priests so much.' In her gentle, innocent, childlike nature opinions and ideas, whether her own or other people's, germinated and spread like tall leafy trees and concealed from her the clear reflection of her own soul.

Mottura used to spend so much time with Balbo that a verb was invented in the office, 'to motture'. 'What is Balbo doing?' 'Oh, he is motturing.' After talking to Mottura, Balbo would go to the Publisher and report to him on Mottura's plans for the scientific books, which were nothing to do with Balbo, but he used to poke his nose into everything and say what he thought and give an opinion in a directionless way. Balbo knew nothing about science. Although he had studied medicine for two years, before he began to read law, he could not remember anything from those two years. In fact, my father, who had been his examiner in anatomy all those years ago, was the only scientist Balbo knew. He felt impelled by his discussions with Mottura to get hold of science books, which he did not read, but into which he poked his red nose, here and there, for a second or two. From his talks with Mottura he was very quick to pick up ideas and judgments. He talked to him for pure pleasure, and not to obtain opinions and suggestions. In talking to people he never had any precise aims, and even if he did at the outset he quickly forgot them. He talked for the sake of disinterested research, quite without purpose, as it were to relieve himself on the publishing house of what he had learnt — like someone who shits because he has to, but at the same time is aware he is fertilizing a field. His way of working would not have been conceivable or tolerated anywhere but in that publishing house. Later he did indeed learn to work differently. But this was how he worked then. When at last he got to bed he felt exhausted. He was writing a book too; but when he found time to

164

write no one could understand. However he did write it because at one point he had it printed. Balbo begged others to correct the proofs as he was a hopeless proof-reader; it took him months and he never spotted mistakes.

I used to stay until quite late in the evening at the Balbos. Three of their friends were always there. One was a little man with a moustache; one looked rather like Gramsci,[41] and the third was a rosy-cheeked, curly-haired man who was always smiling. This man who was always smiling joined the publishing company to work on the scientific books. This seemed odd because he had never had anything to do with any form of science, but evidently he did the work well since he retained the job for years and in fact became the science director — still with that gentle inoffensive smile, his arms spread wide, and maintaining that he knew nothing about science. Finally he left us and set up as a publisher of scientific books on his own account.[42]

When Balbo could spare a moment from discussions he used to expound to Pavese and myself his views on our writing. Pavese sat under the lamp in his armchair, smoking his pipe and listening with a mischievous smile. Whatever Balbo told him Pavese would say he already knew. He listened, though, with lively pleasure. In his relations with us, his friends, there was always an element of teasing. This teasing was one of the nicest things about him, yet he could never laugh about the things he really cared about, or about his relations with women he was in love with, or his books. Friendship was completely natural to him and unstudied, so he did not take it too seriously. He flung himself into love affairs and writing in such a feverish manner that he could never laugh or be entirely himself. At times when I think of him now, teasing is what I most remember, and mourn too, for he is no longer alive. There is not a trace of teasing in his books; the only place where one could see it was in the flash of his mischievous smile.

For myself, I longed to hear my books discussed. Balbo's remarks seemed at times to penetrate like a flash of lightning. At the same time I was fully aware that he only read a few lines of any book. His time-table gave him no time for reading; but he made up for lack of time with a swift acute intuition which enabled him to make a judgment from a few sentences. Sometimes, away from him, I could not help hating his way of forming judgments, and I would accuse him of

165

being superficial. I was wrong: he was anything but vague or superficial. Close and prolonged reading would not have produced a fuller or more deeply considered assessment. Only his practical advice was vague or superficial. The practical advice which he gave me when he commented on my books or saw me depressed was that I should take a more active part in the meetings of the cell or section of the Communist Party to which I belonged at that time. He thought this would bring me into the real world from which he said I was detached. At the time an opinion widely held was that writers ought through the parties of the Left to break out of their patch of shade and mingle with living reality. I was not then in a position to see that this advice was mistaken; I simply felt more unhappy and disorientated. But I obeyed him and went to meetings which, in my innermost soul and without being able to confess the fact, I found cheerless and boring.

I realized later that there was not the slightest need to follow Balbo's advice. His words must not be taken as a practical suggestion, although stripped of any practical implications they were useful and fruitful. But then I felt impelled to follow him step by step, and step by step to make the same mistakes as he made. Pavese made other mistakes on his own account; they were not the same as ours. He stumbled along other paths where he pursued his way alone, disdainfully and obstinately, with his sad and gentle spirit.

The mistakes Pavese made were more serious than ours. Ours were the products of impulse, imprudence, stupidity and honesty. His, on the other hand, were born of foresight, cleverness, calculation and intelligence. Nothing is more dangerous. That sort of mistake can be fatal, as indeed they were for him. It is difficult to retrace one's steps over paths which have been mistakenly chosen through being too clever. Mistakes committed through cleverness tie us in tight knots. Cleverness plants roots which are stronger than those of rash behaviour or imprudence. How are we to free ourselves from those bonds which are so tenacious, so tight and go so deep? Foresight, calculation and cleverness seem reasonable on the face of things; the face, the bitter voice of reason which argues with its infallible arguments, to which there is no answer, and one can only agree.

Pavese killed himself one summer when none of us was in Turin. He had thought out and prepared the circumstances of his death, as one prepares and arranges an excursion or an evening out. He never liked there to be anything unforeseen or accidental in his excursions or evenings out. When he and I, with the Balbos and the Publisher, went for a walk in the hills he was very annoyed if anything upset the arrangements he had made; if someone arrived late at the rendezvous; if we changed our plans on the spur of the moment; if an unexpected person came with us; if some chance led us to eat in the house of an acquaintance we had met on the way instead of in the restaurant selected by him beforehand. The unexpected upset him: he did not like to be taken by surprise.

He had talked for years of killing himself. No one ever believed he would do so. He was already talking of suicide when he came, eating cherries, to see Leone and me when the Germans were over-running France. Not because of France, the Germans, or the war which was overtaking Italy. He was afraid of the war, but not to the extent of committing suicide. As soon as the war was over we began immediately to be afraid of another war, and always to be thinking about it. Only his fear was far greater than ours; it was the culmination of the unforeseen and the unknowable which seemed so horrible to his clear thinking; dark, swirling poisonous waters on the ravished shores of his life.

He had not, in fact, any real motive for killing himself. But he found motives and then added them up with lightning precision. Then he gathered them together and looked again, and agreed, with his mischievous smile, that the total was the same and must be accurate. And he looked beyond his own life to our future and thought how people would react to his books and his memory. He looked beyond death, like those people who are in love with life and cannot detach themselves from it, and by thinking about death come to imagine it not as death but as life. He, however, was not in love with life. That way of looking beyond his own death was not love for life, but a quick calculation of circumstances made so that nothing, even after he was dead, could take him by surprise.

BALBO left the publishing house and went to live in Rome. For years he vacillated between various absurd projects and false starts. Finally he got a proper job and learnt to work like other people. Nevertheless he would still forget meal-times, and just as he had done as a publisher, would forget to leave when the office emptied. In fact he worked harder than other people without realizing it, and in the evening was astonished to find himself exhausted.

The Balbos now had three children, and were trying to be conventional parents, of which they were both incapable, and which weighed on them. They were wont to accuse each other every day of being inadequate. Neither could grasp how to bring up children, but each called on the other to be what the other was not. Balbo tried to teach his children the one thing that he knew well, and that was geography; he remembered nothing at all about other school subjects, although according to his own account, he had been an excellent pupil.

He never discussed history with them, partly because he did not know any and partly because he was afraid of introducing his own judgments and political opinions into historical facts. He did not want to offer his children cut and dried judgments. He felt that they ought to form their own judgments and opinions. This seems strange in a man like himself who had been for so long aggressive and assertive in imparting his opinions to his friends, and equally aggressive and assertive in receiving opinions from others — that is to say in adopting the opinions of others as his own, recasting and remodelling them and giving them the hallmark of his own thought. But with his children he showed himself as cautious as could be in serving up the food of his thoughts.

So Lola and her husband never talked politics in their children's presence. She refrained because she disliked sectarianism, he because he thought one should avoid complex discussions with children. And since they were each afraid of confusing them and making them diffident and uncertain in the face of established authority, they never mentioned the story of 'jug' in front of the children. Lola, in particular, had dreamed up a model family of children which she constantly compared with her own idle, undisciplined and inattentive children. In fact she never stopped scolding them in a rough and chaotic manner. This frightened no one but it made the house feel vaguely uneasy, noisy and messy. At the same time she invented an ideal husband and father, quite different from what Balbo was or could ever set out to be, and from time to time she screamed at her husband and her children with a long throaty cry of exasperation, like the one with which once she had used to complain about the people who thronged her house.

Their house in Rome — unlike their previous home in the Corso Re Umberto in Turin — was not full of visitors. Instead they now had few friends who called at reasonable hours, people to whom, at times, Balbo had nothing special to say, with whom he would be silent for a time, or just chat playfully. The old overmastering urge to talk had been appeased. He now directed his mind to specific ends, steered it to specific persons at preordained times, retreating later into silence much as one closes the shutters in the evenings.

Occasionally when travelling alone or when the children had gone away for the holidays, Balbo and his wife enjoyed themselves as they used to, they relaxed at leisure, dawdled in the streets, where he made her buy dresses and shoes that pleased him, or they went dancing at night clubs.

In the end Lola took a job as well. She didn't choose it: it fell at her feet when she wasn't looking for work. It was possibly not the job she would have chosen, and it bore no resemblance at all to 'jug' — that is, the time which she reckoned as the best and the most exalted of her life. However, she succeeded in doing this work well and in using her intelligence. She also brought to it her untidiness, impatience and restlessness, and her zest for quarrels. This particular zest found another outlet, especially at the post office where sometimes she had to despatch pamphlets and parcels as part of her job.

She worked for a group of lawyers — usually at home: she shouted orders to the daily and to the children, telephoned her mother-in-law, and had herself measured for dresses. This job piled chaos on top of chaos. Sometimes she had to do up parcels, and then she would suddenly decide that the children should do them up, having on the spur of the moment formed a picture of skilful children, who were good at wrapping up parcels. She would shout 'Luucaaa!' and Luca would appear, a large child, covered with ink-stains, and lost in a fog of idleness, slow and indifferent as a prince, and she told him to pack up some twenty parcels, at once. Luca had never made a parcel in his life. She put a sheaf of wrapping-paper and a ball of string in his hands. Luca wandered about the house with the string, lazily absorbed, and having quite forgotten, aimlessly dawdling around until she descended on him, yelling, and snatched the string out of his hands, and he gazed at her with his proud green expressionless eyes from the depths of his princely silence.

The Balbos always went skiing in the winter. They now took the children with them. They had, however, to come up North since they despised the low, windy, overcrowded mountains outside Rome. They went to Sestrières or even Switzerland. There on the snow-slopes Lola was free. She forgot her lawyers, the children's lessons, the daily who was probably using too much oil, her bad moods and her eternal resentment. But in order to gain that freedom the preceding days in Rome had to be endured; days of uncontrollable chaos, suitcases packed and unpacked, jerseys mislaid, shouting, breathless dashing all over the city, orders given and cancelled, with the daily woman completely bewildered, and Luca inscrutably covered with inkstains, the telephone ringing, and appointments with her lawyers.

In the summer Lola also went to bathe at Ostia, alone, because her husband was not fond of the sea and her sons were by then as a rule out of Rome at Boy Scout camps. She went with casual acquaintances whom she made use of quite simply for the purpose of having herself fetched and brought home again in their cars. Her conversations with these casual acquaintances neither bored nor amused her. She had a social side to her, unconnected with either boredom or amusement, but usually linked with an immediate purpose, such as being taken somewhere in a car, or obtaining the addresses of upholsterers that were miles away, carpenters who cost very little but were not on the telephone, or drapers at the other end of the world, where she was able, thanks to these casual acquaintances, to get small discounts.

By the sea at Ostia she enjoyed herself on her own. She swam a long way out, dried off in the sun, and tanned herself to an improbable brown, although her doctors had advised her not to stay in the sun too long because of an illness she had once had, of which she was still very frightened, but not enough to keep her away from the sea and sun and sand. She returned for lunch at four o'clock and the house echoed with that affectionate guttural cry for her husband. She felt pacified by her morning of freedom and leisure. She loved the summer, the heat, and having her sons away camping, and being able to wander round the house in a bathing-dress and with bare feet.

I was still living in Turin, but I frequently went to Rome and was preparing to go and live there permanently. I had married again and my husband[43] was teaching in Rome. We were looking for a house there. In a little while I would bring the children down and we would be installed in Rome for good. I went to see the Balbos. We had always remained friends and were talking about old times. I said to Balbo: 'Do you remember when we used to do "self-criticism"?'

We used to do a lot of 'self-criticism' in the years immediately after the war. That is to say, after having made mistakes we analysed and dissected them at the tops of our voices. We piled mistakes on mistakes, and self-criticism was then superimposed on the mistakes and was interposed and blended with them. It was rather like the way in which music blended with words in an opera, veiling the meaning and carrying them off in its own glorious rhythm. I said: 'Do you remember when we used to hold political meetings?'

When Lola recalled her husband's election speeches she still groaned in pain. She could see him there once more, a little man on wooden hustings with flags flapping round him, and the piazza below thronged with people, while he strung sentences together in an indecisive voice, scratching the top of his head with his forefinger. The cold dark night came on, and he was still stringing sentences together, absorbed in following the tortuous, subtle train of his own thoughts, convinced that the people listening were following his confused meanderings. People waited in vain for the ringing slogans they were used to hearing. But they cheered all the same, albeit out of good-will and unimpaired confidence, or possibly so that he should finally finish talking.

My father also once delivered an election speech during those years. They had asked him to add his name to the list of candidates for the Popular Front, in which Communists and Socialists presented themselves together. He had consented. They told him that he ought to address at least one meeting, just one only, and he was invited to

171

talk about whatever he liked. He was taken to a theatre, and there on the stage my father began his electoral address: 'Science is the quest for truth!'

He spoke of nothing but science for some twenty minutes and the audience maintained a stupefied silence. He said at one point that scientific research in America was in advance of that in Russia. The audience, more bewildered than ever, remained silent. However, in one place he mentioned quite incidentally the name of Mussolini, whom he used to call 'the ass of Predappio'. Thereupon a roar of applause broke loose, and my father gazed about him in stupefaction, bewildered in his turn. That was my father's election speech.

Balbo had been present at this meeting and laughed to recall the scene. He liked my father very much, and remembered those two years he had spent reading medicine. At the beginning of the academic year there used to be ragging at the gate of the Institute, and fights with the new students. Balbo would describe how my father put his head down and butted into the crowd like a buffalo charging into a herd in order to force his way through.

I can remember my father careering along with his head down like a buffalo during the war, when an air-raid caught him in the street. He did not go down into the shelters, but when the alarm sounded he started running for home. Amid the roar of aircraft and the whistling of bombs he ran with his head down, close to the walls, quite happy, because danger was a thing he loved.

'Fools,' he would say later. 'Fancy me going into a shelter! A lot dying matters to me.'

WHEN I told my mother that I would be leaving Turin and settling in Rome, she was very displeased. 'You are taking away my little ones from me,' she said. 'You really are a cow!'

'She will send them out in rags,' she said to Miranda, 'she will send them out without buttons. Out at the seat!'

She recalled visiting me in internment, I had a basket in the kitchen with all the things to be mended in it, but I never finished them. I started to sew for a bit and then put the work down. 'I can't sew any more. I have lost the needle.'

For many years now I had not had a house of my own, no linen cupboard, nor a basket for the things to be mended, so consequently nothing got done. For years I lived with my father and mother, and it was my mother who looked after everything.

In the summer it was my father and mother who took the children to the mountains, usually to Perlotoa where they rented the same old house with a lawn in front. I remained alone in the city and didn't leave it except for a few days when the publishing business closed down. 'We are going for a walk,' my father would say early in the morning in the mountains. He was dressed in his old rust-coloured jacket, long socks and hob-nailed boots. 'Up you get, come along. We are going for a walk. You mustn't get lazy. I won't have you always lying on that lawn.'

We used to come back in September. My mother then summoned Tersilla to make trousers, overalls for school, pyjamas and overcoats.

'I want them neat. I like to keep children neat. All their little things must be ready. It is such a comfort to think that they are nice and warm.'

In the evening she used to read Sans Famille[44] to the children. 'Sans Famille is so lovely,' she would say. 'It is one of the best books there are. Marchesa Colombi's books were lovely too. It's a pity they are not still available; you ought to tell your Publisher to reprint the Marchesa Colombi's books. They were lovely.'

I had given the children Misunderstood.[45] Paola had read it to me

173

when I was very young. At that time she loved books with an unhappy ending, that were sad and moving and made one cry. My mother did not like *Misunderstood,* she found it too sad.

'*Sans Famille* is nicer,' she said, 'there is no comparison. *Misunderstood* is too sentimental. I don't like it very much. But *Sans Famille*! Capi! Monsieur Vitali! The swaddling clothes lied, Honour thy father and thy mother. The swaddling clothes told the truth!' And she would continue to enumerate the characters in *Sans Famille* and the chapter-headings which she knew by heart, having read the book several times to her own children, now she was reading it to mine, a chapter an evening, and she still fell under the spell of those ups and downs which at times took a dramatic turn, but never ended unhappily. She fell under the spell of the dog Capi. She was fond of dogs and had a particularly soft spot for Capi. 'I should love to have a dog like that. But just imagine Papa allowing me to have one. I should like to have a real lion too! I like lions so much. All wild animals!' she said.

She used to hurry off to a circus whenever she could and make an excuse to take the children too. 'I am sorry there is no zoo in Turin; I should go there every day. I am always so keen to see a lovely wild animal.

'*Misunderstood,* no, it is not so good. Paola liked it when she was a girl. She and Mario had a mania for unhappy things. Now, fortunately, they have grown out of that.'

'Mario and Paola formed a grand alliance when they were young,' my father said. 'Do you remember when they were always whispering with poor Terni? They were mad on Proust and talked about nothing else. Now Paola and Mario have cooled off, they never look at one another. He finds her bourgeois. What asses!'

'When is your translation of Proust coming out?' my mother asked. 'It is some time now since I have read him. But I remember it, it is wonderful! I remember Madame Verdurin! Odette! Swann! Madame Verdurin must have been rather like Drusilla.'

When I married again, and after a while went to live in Rome, my mother bore a grudge against me for some time. But this grudge never became bitterly or deeply rooted in her heart. I travelled back and forth between Rome and Turin and was preparing to leave Turin for ever. I said goodbye, in my heart, to the publishing house, and to the city. I intended to continue working for the company in Rome, though I felt that it would be different. I loved the office on the Corso Re Umberto, a few yards from the Café Platti, a few yards from the house where the Balbos were when they still lived in Turin, and a few yards from the hotel under the arcades where Pavese had died.

I had loved my colleagues at work, but those ones, not others. I felt that I should not be able to work among another lot of people. And in fact when I was in Rome in the end I left the firm as I was incapable of working without the Publisher and my former colleagues.

My husband, Gabriele, wrote to me from Rome urging me to hurry up and come down with the children. He had made friends with the Balbos and went to them in the evenings when he was alone.

'But in Rome you must learn to darn,' my mother said. 'Or else you must find a woman who is good at darning. Find a dressmaker who will come to the house, someone like Tersilla. Ask Lola. Lola is sure to know a dressmaker who comes for the day. Or ask Adele Rasetti. Go and see Adele, she is so nice. I am so fond of Adele.'

'Make a note of Adele's address,' said my father. 'I will write it down for you. Don't lose it. I'll give you my cousin's address, too, poor Ettore's son. He is a very good doctor. You can call him.'

'Mind you go at once to see Adele,' my father said. 'Woe betide you if you don't. I don't want you to make an ass of yourself. Apart from Gino, you lot all make asses of yourselves with people. Mario is an ass. He must have been a complete ass with Frances when she went to see him in Paris. He can't have given her a chance. And she gave me to understand that his house was very untidy, as usual.'

'To think that Mario was once so tidy!' my mother said. 'He was so meticulous and boring. He was like Silvio.'

'But now,' said my father, 'he has changed. Frances told me it was a mess there. You lot are all a real mess.'

'Except me,' said my mother. 'I am tidy. Look at my cupboards.'

'What? You muddle everything up! You couldn't find my winter suit.'

'Oh yes I could. I knew perfectly well where it was. But I had put it aside to give away. It's old and you can't wear it any more, Beppino.'

'You think I'm going to throw it out! I shouldn't dream of it. Can you see me getting a new suit!'

'You last had one made when you went to Liège. You wore it all

175

through the war. You have been wearing it for nearly ten years now.'

'What does it matter how long I've been wearing it, it is still a very good suit. I don't throw money away like you lot. You lot are all megalomaniacs.' My poor mama too was always insisting I should get clothes made. She didn't want me to look bad when I went to La Vendée's. My cousin, poor Ettorino, was very well-dressed, and she didn't want me to make a poor show beside him. At La Vendée's there used to be dinner for fifty or sixty guests. There was a train of carriages. Bepo, her man, waited at table. Once he fell down some steps and broke a huge pile of plates. When poor Cesare, my brother, weighed himself after one of those dinners he had put on five or six kilos. He was too fat, my poor brother Cesare. He ate too much. Alberto eats such a lot: I shouldn't like him to become as fat as poor Cesare. They all ate too much. People ate too much in those days. I remember my grandmother Dolcetta; what a lot she used to eat. My poor mama, on the other hand, ate little; she was thin. As a young woman she was very beautiful; she had a very beautiful head. Everybody said that she had a very beautiful head. She too used to give dinners for fifty or sixty people. There were ices with hot sauce. They ate very well. My cousin Regina was extremely smart at those dinners. She was beautiful, Regina, very beautiful.'

'No, Beppino,' said my mother, 'she was not really beautiful.'

'Oh no, you are wrong, she was very beautiful. I liked her very much, so did poor Cesare. All the same, as a young woman, she was a bit flighty, very flighty. Even my mama always said that Regina was very flighty.'

'My uncle, the Lunatic, sometimes used to go to your mama's dinners too,' said my mother.

'Sometimes. Um, but not always. The Lunatic rather put on airs. He found the atmosphere there bourgeois, reactionary. Your uncle tended to put on airs.'

'He was so nice,' said my mother. 'The Lunatic was so nice, such fun. He was like Silvio; Silvio took after him.'

' "My good Signor Lipmann". Do you remember how he used to say that,' my mother said. 'And then he always said, "Blessed are the orphans!" He used to say that many lunatics had gone mad through their parents' fault. "Blessed are the orphans," he was always saying. In fact he had worked out psychoanalysis although it had not been invented yet.'

176

' "My good Signor Lipmann", ' said my mother. 'I can almost hear him still.'

'My poor mama,' said my father, 'kept a carriage. She went out for a drive in it every day. She always took Gino and Mario and after a while they began to be sick because the smell of leather upset them. They messed up the whole carriage and she was very cross about it. Poor dear woman! She was so very sorry when she had to part with the carriage.

'Poor Mama. When I came back from Spitzbergen where I had been inside the whale's skull looking for the cerebro-spinal ganglia, I had my clothes in a bag with me, all filthy with whales' blood, and she was too disgusted to touch them, so I took them up to the attic where they stank horribly. I never found the cerebro-spinal ganglia, and my mama said, "He has ruined good clothes for nothing!" '

'Perhaps you didn't look for them properly,' my mother said. 'Perhaps you ought to have looked a bit harder.'

'What!' my father said. 'What a silly woman you are. It wasn't exactly easy. You are always ready to put me down. What an ass you are!'

'When I was at my boarding-school,' said my mother, 'I studied whales too. Natural history was taught well, and I liked it very much. But at that school we had to go to Mass too often; we were always having to go to confession. Sometimes we really had no sin to confess, and then we used to say "I have stolen the snow!" "I have stolen the snow." Ah, my school was so nice. I did enjoy myself!' Every Sunday I went to see Whiskers. We called his sisters "the Blessed Ones" because they were very devout. Whiskers' real name was Perego and his friends made up a rhyme about him, which went:

By day, by night, we have a merry-go
At the house and cellar of our Perego.'

'Oh, don't let us start on Whiskers now,' my father said. 'I have heard that story so many times.'

177

Notes

1. *Leonida Bissolati* (1857–1920)   A prominent moderate member of the Italian Socialist Party, he favoured intervention on the Allied side in World War I. Decorated for bravery on the Italian front; a street is named after him in Rome.

2   *Filippo Turati*   Born the same year as Bissolati, he was the founder of Italian Socialism (1st Congress 1892). Exiled to France in 1926, he became the leader in Paris of the Italian anti-Fascist movement. He died there in 1932: his testament a sonnet in which he asked that no headstone be placed or priestly rites performed where his ashes lay scattered, but that young people should gather there to discourse of happiness and love.

3   *Anna Kulischova*   Born in Moscow in 1957, fled to Switzerland in 1877 to escape police harassment over her revolutionary activities. Met Andrea Costa, eventually parted from him and was associated with Turati, practising medicine among the poor in Milan. Their house was for many years the centre of the freshest energies in Italian Socialism. She died in 1925.

4   *Il baco del calo del malo*   A children's word-game in which the words are repeated with different vowels — *baco, bico, beco,* etc — until the phrase becomes *il buco del culo del mulo,* which is surprisingly vulgar (in English 'the hole of the arse of the mule').

5   *Andreina Costa*   Daughter of Anna Kulischova and Andrea Costa (see notes 3 and 6).

6   *Andrea Costa*   Husband of Anna Kulischova (3) and father of Andreina Costa (5). An anarchist in his youth, he later became a Socialist and eventually a Liberal.

7   *Felice Casorati*   A contemporary painter.

8   *Ettore Petrolini*   The best known and most beloved Italian comedian during and after the Fascist era. Died in Rome in 1963.

9   *Giacomo de Benedetti*   A literary critic.

10   *Giancarlo Pajetta*   Prominent Communist Resistance fighter, and Member of Parliament. Entrusted with the Party's foreign affairs section.

11 *La Stampa* The most important middle-class newspaper apart from *Il Corriere della Sera*. Published in Turin.

12 *Adriano Olivetti* Son of the founder of the typewriter firm, Camillo Olivetti (1868–1943). Notable for his interest in industrial welfare and design.

13 *Carlo Rosselli* (1899–1937) In his early twenties he became a devoted follower of Matteotti, the Socialist Leader of the Opposition in Mussolini's parliament, whose murder in 1925 by Fascist gangsters spelt the end of democracy in Italy. Rosselli fled to France where he founded the anti-Fascist political movement 'Giustizia e Libertà', to which all the Italian exiles belonged. In his turn he was assassinated by order of Mussolini, together with his brother.

14 *Ferruccio Parri* Prominent statesman and anti-Fascist politician. Led the first post-war Italian Government. Life Senator.

15 *Vittorio Foa* Prominent Socialist politician and trade unionist.

16 *Luigi Salvatorelli* Distinguished writer, teacher and liberal leader.

17 *Mario Vinciguerra* (born 1887) A well-known anti-Fascist. Author of *Romanticismo, I Partiti Politici Italiani 1848–1955*, and *Croce*.

18 *Ricardo Bauer* (born 1896) Editor of the anti-Fascist *Non Mollare*. Imprisoned by the Fascists. A member of the Action Party.

19 *Ernesto Rossi* (1897–1967) Economist and journalist. Imprisoned under the Fascists, 1930–43. Involved in the 'Giustizia e Libertà' movement and an executive of the Action Party. A minister in Parri's coalition government at the end of the war.

20 *Guglielmo Ferrero* (1871–1942) Journalist, historian and sociologist. an anglophile and opponent of the Libyan war. Signed Croce's anti-Fascist manifesto in 1925.

21 *Pitigrilli* (1893–1975) Pseudonym of Sion Segre. A popular writer of highly-coloured romances, very successful in the 1920s.

22 *Carlo Levi* Painter and writer, born in Turin in 1902. Close friend of Piero Gobetti, whose new liberalism was to be influential among anti-Fascists but who died in 1926, aged 25. Levi received medical training. Arrested several times, he was confined to the malaria-infested village of Gagliano 1935–6. *Cristo si è fermato a Eboli (Christ stopped at Eboli*, London 1948) was his indictment of social conditions there. In France 1939–44, where he helped to found 'Giustizia e Libertà'; then a resistance leader in Tuscany. Edited *Italia Libera*, the Action Party paper, 1945–6. Author of *Paura della Liberta (Of Fear and Freedom*, London 1950) and the novel *L'Orologio (The Watch*, London 1952).

23 *Giulio Einaudi* (born 1912) Son of Luigi Einaudi, Liberal economist and President of Italy (1948–55). Founder and head of the Turin

publishing firm which maintained a covert hostility to Fascism under Mussolini. Publisher of Natalia Ginzburg's works.

24 *Cesare Pavese* (1908–1950)   One of the most important post-war Italian writers. As an anti-Fascist he felt restricted to translation and critical essays at first. Arrested in 1935. With partisans in his native Piedmont from 1943. As a writer he combined a romantic temperament with political commitment to Communism. His best known novels are *Il Compagno (The Comrade*, London 1959), *Tra Donne Sole (Among Women Only*, London 1948) and *La Luna e i Falo (The Moon and the Bonfire*, London 1952). He also wrote some notable love lyrics. *Lavorare Stanco (A Mania for Solitude: selected poems 1930–1950*, trs. Margaret Crosland, London 1969).

25 *Giovanni Pascoli* (1855–1912)   A tragic poet, born in Romagna. Imprisoned for socialist agitation as a student. Professor of Latin at Bologna from 1907.

26 *Giosuè Carducci* (1835–1907)   A lyric poet, born near Pisa. Professor of Italian Literature, Bologna, 1860. Republican Deputy, 1876. Senator, 1890. Awarded Nobel Prize, 1906.

27 *Giacomo Leopardi* (1798–1837)   The most important Italian lyric poet of the nineteenth century; scholar in several languages. An invalid from his twenties till his early death.

28 *Enrico Fermi* (1904–54)   Major contributor to theoretical and experimental nuclear physics. Awarded the Nobel Prize 1938 and, being a Jew, emigrated to the USA, where his work led to the first controlled nuclear chain reaction. Assisted in the development of the atomic bomb at Los Alamos from 1942. Died at the height of his powers.

29 *Benedetto Croce* (1866–1957)   Philosopher, historian, critic. Founded the review *La Critica* in 1903, which continued for forty-one years. Developed a phenomenology of mind in opposition to Hegel, synthesizing ethics, politics and aesthetics. Tended to regard liberalism and democracy as incompatible and discounted the dangers of Fascism until 1925, when he promoted a manifesto of dissent. Served in coalition of 1944 and helped to revive democracy.

30 *Felice Balbo* (1912–64)   anti-Fascist writer and teacher. Exponent of a left-wing Catholic position.

31 *Emilio Salgari* (1862–1911)   Author of popular adventure stories.

32 *Nigra sum sed formosa*   'I am black but comely' (Song of Solomon 1:5), black merely indicating a dark complexion.

33 *Rari nantes*   'Apparent rari nantes in gurgite vasto ('Rare swimmers in the vast flood'), Virgil, *Aeneid*, i.118.

34   *Emilio Lussu* (1899–1975)   Writer and politician, exiled from Fascism in France. Helped to found 'Giustizia e Libertà' movement. Member of post-war constituent assembly, Socialist minister and Senator.

35   *The Devourers*   A novel by Annie Vivanti, first published in England in 1910.

36   *Giuseppe Saragat* (born 1898)   Leader of the reformist Socialists, temporarily united with Nenni's maximalists in exile. Secretary of the Italian Socialist Labour Party 1947–64, President of Italy 1964–71, President of the Social Democratic Party from 1975.

37   *Pietro Nenni* (1891–1980)   Socialist politician, born in Romagna. Exiled by the Fascists in 1926, Political commissar with the Spanish Republicans in the Civil War. Secretary-General of the Socialist Party from 1944. Ended alliance with the Communists in 1956. Foreign Minister and then vice-premier in centre-left coalitions of the 1960s.

38   *Palmiro Togliatti* (1890–1964)   Ran the weekly *L'Ordine Nuovo* with Gramsci (41). Both broke away from the Socialist Party in 1921 to found the Communist Party. Togliatti was Secretary-General from his exile in 1922 until his death. Served in Spain 1937–9, was then in Russia until 1944. Minister for Justice in the post-war coalition until the end of de Gasperi's first Cabinet.

39   *Partito D'Azione* (Action Party)   Originated in 1942–3 from the 'Giustizia e Libertà' movement, which played a large part in the Resistance: an attempt at a non-clerical, non-Socialist third force. Disbanded after its comparative failure in the 1948 elections.

40   *Luisa Ferida* (1914–45)   A film actress who collaborated with the Germans and was shot by partisans in 1945.

41   *Antonio Gramsci* (1891–1937)   See note 38. An immensely influential writer; he helped to found the Italian Communist Party. Deputy 1924. Arrested 1926 and died in confinement.

42   The publishing house referred to is Paolo Boringhieri, Turin.

43   *Gabriele Baldini* (1919–69)   Professor of English Literature at the University of Rome. Fellow of Trinity College, Cambridge, 1948–50. Author of works on Melville, Webster and Shakespeare.

44   *Sans Famille*   The story of a foundling boy by the French children's writer, Hector Malo, published 1879. (*Nobody's Boy,* English translation by Florence Crewe-Jones).

45   *Misunderstood*   A very popular but mawkish children's story of 1869, by Florence Montgomery.